Jamen's Yuletide Bride

A Gwyn Brothers Novella

Fairelle Series Book 2.5

By Rebekah R. Ganiere

ISBN: 978-1-63300-004-9
ISBN: 978-1-63300-005-6
Cover art by Rebekah R. Ganiere
Photography by Cory Stierley

Fallen Angel Press
1040 N. Las Palmas Blvd.
Bldg. 24 Suite 203
Los Angeles, CA 90038
www.FallenAngelPress.com

FALLEN
ANGEL
PRESS

Ordering Information:
Orders by U.S. trade bookstores and wholesalers. Please visit
www.FallenAngelPress.com.
Printed in the United States of America

DEDICATION
For my amazing Critique Partners, Beta Readers
And for The Bitten

Tanah Darah

Shaidan

Daemon Wastelands

Wolvenglen

Rift

Sage's Hideout

Ruins

Snow's Cottage

Volkzene

Westfall

Belle's Cottage

Gwyn Manor

Morlain

Abandoned Castle

Ville DeFee

Zelle's Tower

Draak Land

Ryna's Lake

Wizard Towers

Verdenalla

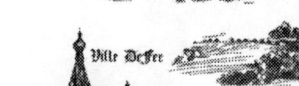

Pereum, Fairelle Year 200
PROLOGUE

In the year 200, in the city of Pereum, the heart of Fairelle, King Isodor lay on his deathbed. With all of Fairelle united under his banner, his four rival sons vied for the crown. One-by-one, the brothers called forth a djinn named Xereus from Shaidan, the daemon realm, to grant a single wish. But Xereus tricked the brothers, twisting their wishes.

The eldest wished to forever be bloodthirsty in battle, and was thus transformed into a Vampire. The second wished for the unending loyalty of his men, and was turned into a Werewolf. The third asked for the ability to manipulate the elements of Fairelle; he became physically weak, but mighty in magick, a Fae. And the last asked to rule the sea. A Nereid.

When the king died, each brother took a piece of Fairelle for himself and waged war for control of the rest. Xereus, having been called forth so many times, tore a rift between his daemonic plane and Fairelle, allowing thousands of daemons to pour into Pereum.

Years upon years of bloody warring went by, all races fighting for control, and eventually the daemons gained dominion of the heart of Fairelle. Realizing that all lands would soon fall into the daemons' control, the High Elders of the Fae and the Mages from the south combined their magicks to seal the rift. The daemons were banished back to their own plane, but Pereum was wiped off the map in the process, leaving only charred waste behind, forever, known as The Daemon Wastelands.

Upon the day of the rift closing, a Mage soothsayer prophesied of the healing of Fairelle. Over the next thousand years, the races continued to war against each other, waiting for the day when the ancient prophesies would begin.

Nine prophesies, a thousand years old, to unite the lands and heal Fairelle.

Among the prophesies were mentioned the return of Vampire Slayers. The seven Gwyn Brothers were chosen to be Vampire Slayers. To protect their lands of Westfall from the monsters that lay beyond. And to keep all of Fairelle from falling prey to the evil that lurks in the shadows.

Westfall Village, 1208 A.D. (After Daemons)

CHAPTER ONE

Scarlet brushed her hair and smiled to herself. She was going to marry the man she loved. She'd waited for Jamen to ask her ever since the first time he'd come into her father's store in his fine tan tunic and black breeches, with his curls dangling in his chestnut brown eyes. In that moment she'd known that her heart would never belong to another.

Last night, when they'd made love for the first time, had been the happiest moment of her life. Never before had he kissed her with so much need, or touched her like she was so precious. The weight of his hips on hers and the feel of their bodies joined had been bliss beyond what she thought the world capable of. Jamen Gwyn was her soul mate and soon they would be wed and he'd be hers alone, forever.

She closed her eyes remembering the intimate hours they'd spent together in her bed as her parents had been out. Her skin flushed and arousal gripped her tight. Would it happen again before they married? It shouldn't. It wasn't proper. But she and Jamen had never been accused of being proper. Even though he was a young Lord of Gwyn manor, he was fourth in line to inherit, so he wasn't bound by the same rules as his older brothers.

Male voices floated up the stairs and in through Scarlet's door, pulling her attention away from her happiness. Her gaze travelled to the wooden clock on the mantle. It was just after ten and the moon shone high in the night sky.

She set down her brush on her antique vanity and rose from her seat. Gathering the hem of her long chemise she tiptoed to the top of the stairs.

"No, I need...I need to s–see her now."

Scarlet frowned at the sound of Jamen's voice.

"Lord Gwyn," her father said. "This is most improper. It is late and you are... inebriated M'lord. Mayhaps it would be best if you spoke to Scarlet tomorrow."

There was a scuffling sound and then Jamen appeared at the bottom of the stairs. Scarlet's heartbeat quickened and a trickle of fear raced up her neck. His hair was disheveled and his tunic lay open and untucked revealing the chiseled chest that had pressed down upon her the previous night. One of the legs of his breeches was tucked into his boot the other was not. Jamen was always immaculate in his appearance. From the sight of his appearance she knew something was wrong.

"Sssssscarlet," he slurred. "I need to talk...I need to talk to you."

"All right."

Her father appeared at Jamen's shoulder, wringing his hands.

She descended the stairs in a slow deliberate step. Her knees wobbled and she clung to the banister.

"It's all right father. We'll speak in the den," she said.

Her father continued to wring his hands; his mouth opening and closing like a giant coddlefish.

She was two stairs from Jamen when the stench of alcohol hit her. She'd never seen him so low. They occasionally spent time together with friends at the inn and he would drink, but never like this. Her throat tightened.

"Come." She tried to clear her gravelly throat but couldn't. She pointed to the door on the right. Jamen continued to stare at her for a minute. His glassy, unfocused eyes took her in. He blinked several times and then nodded. Swaying, he leaned on the wall for support as he made his way to the room.

He flung himself into a large stuffed chair and hung his head in his hands. Scarlet stepped in followed by her father. She wished to tell her father to leave, whatever was wrong was none of her father's business, but she couldn't. Somehow his presence at her back strengthened her.

She stood silently waiting. Her heart pounded and her hands shook.

When Jamen didn't speak she walked over to him. Her body moving as disjointedly as a scarecrow. He didn't look up, so she knelt and placed her hands on his knees. He finally lifted his gaze.

His eyes were bloodshot. Deep purpled circles bruised the skin underneath. He stank of liquor and sweat. He stared at her for a long time, saying nothing. Anxiety twisted and turned under her skin, almost consuming her. Jamen wasn't a man of many words and to force him to speak would do no good, but the longer he sat staring, the shakier she became.

He picked up her hands in his. His thumb rolled across the back of her fingers caressing her skin and sending butterflies flipping in her belly. Memories of the feel of his lips worshipping her skin, made the her cheeks heat.

"I'm sorry," he whispered. A tear dripped onto her hand and rolled off the side.

Those weren't the words she'd expected and suddenly she didn't want to know.

"For what?" She barely managed to get the words out.

He looked up again, his eyes full of pain and sorrow. He choked on a sob. "I…I love you, Lettie. I love you more than I've ever loved anything. I never thought I'd ever love someone the way that I love you, but I do. So I can't— I won't—" He shook his head and drooped.

The spot where he traced her skin no longer soothed her, but had become like the scratching of a spider crawling across her. She wanted to pull her hands away. Instead she squeezed his fingers tight.

She didn't want to ask. Didn't want to hear, but she had to know. "You can't what, Jamen?"

"I...I can't marry you."

A buzzing started in her ears. An annoying buzz that drowned out her surroundings. Her head lightened, as if she wasn't really in her body anymore. She took in several deep breaths through her nose in an effort to rid herself of the sensations that now plagued her.

It wasn't possible. They'd been together for six years. Laughing, kissing, touching. Falling in love. And last night, he'd told her that he couldn't live without her. That she was his forever. Last night...

She wanted to run to her room, lock her door and pretend that Jamen wasn't in front of her looking like a drunkard. To wake up in the morning and forget that he'd been there.

"I don't think I heard you right," she whispered.

Tears dripped onto her hands again. His chin quivered.

"I can't marry you, Lettie. I want to. I love you and I wish I could, but I can't."

A cold chill swept over her and rooted in her breast. Everything around her ceased to exist. Her mind cleared and her voice came out strong and cold. "I don't understand. Has something happened?"

"No. Yes. I... I can't tell you."

"Let me get you home. You've had too much to drink. We'll talk to Erik–"

"No." Jamen's head shook heavily from side to side. "I don't want to talk to my brothers."

"But maybe they can help–"

"No!" His voice was so forceful that it made her jump.

Jamen never yelled at her.

"My brothers can't help. I'm sorry Lettie. So sorry."

This couldn't be happening. Had she done something? She slid her hands from his grip. "But last night—"

His eyes pleaded with her. "I'm sorry—"

"Yes, you've said that already." The iciness in her heart spread to her limbs. Her knees ached from kneeling.

"Please, forgive me." His tearful eyes pleaded with her.

 She couldn't forgive him.

She stood and backed away. He spoke common tongue but his words made no sense. Anger and anguish whipped through her. How could he do this?

"Forgive you? You come to my home, late at night, reeking of alcohol and tell me you're sorry but you cannot marry me and then ask me to forgive you?" She hugged herself tightly afraid that if she didn't she'd break into a million pieces. "Tell me why, Jamen. *Why* can't you marry me?"

"I...I can't tell you. I want to, I do, but I can't."

Scarlet clenched her jaw and nodded. "Fine." Her voice sounded as hollow as the sermons Father Ohana gave on Sundays.

Removing the emerald ring from her finger she flung it at him. He flinched and stood, reaching for her.

"Lettie, please."

"Leave." Her body quaked at the words. She'd given him everything. Her youth, her innocence, her heart. She'd be ruined. She had the dress, the invitations were ready to be sent out.

He was leaving her. The man she'd given her life to.

"Lettie—"

"Stop calling me that!" she screamed. Her breath whooshed in and out in short, heavy bursts. Her father wrapped his arms around her shoulders, but his touch made her want to scream all the more.

"I think you should go, Lord Gwyn," he said.

Jamen looked between the two and then picked up the ring from the floor. He stared at it in his hand and then his beautiful chestnut eyes travelled to Scarlet. The eyes she'd immersed herself in for the past years. She pressed her nails into her palms to keep from reaching for him.

He took a step forward, the glaze gone from his eyes. "Scarlet—"

"Goodbye, Lord Gwyn," she said formally. She bit the inside of her cheek. She'd given him everything and he was throwing her away like yesterday's waste. The only thing she had left was her pride and she refused to allow him to strip her of that as well.

He stumbled past her, crashing into a table and knocking a vase to the floor. He stopped and looked back, opening his mouth but instead, he turned and fled from the room. The slam of the front door was like a slam through her heart. She stared at the door for a long time, unable to move. In that moment, she vowed to never again allow herself to be made so low by a man.

Gwyn Manor, Westfall, Fairelle
CHAPTER TWO

Three years later

Jamen threw his satchel and saddlebag down onto the wooden table in the solar and let out a deep sigh. His breath hung in the cold air for a moment before disappearing. He scanned the room, knowing every surface by heart. Silence emanated from Gwyn manor. Born and raised in the house, he'd never once heard it that quiet.

It had been months since he'd been home. After Flint's disappearance and his sister Snow's wedding to Sage, he and the rest of his brothers had taken turns coming back from Tanah Darah and lording over the lands that had been in their family for over a hundred years.

Spending time in the vampire homelands of Tanah Darah had been a change for all of them, but Sage and Snow needed the help. The royal guard were mostly dead and even though Sage was now

11

legitimately the King of the Vampires, enemies were still within their ranks. Jamen and his brothers were the best defense Sage and Snow had and it was currently their job to hunt down the vampires who wouldn't obey the new law forbidding the feeding off non-consenting humans.

Though the brothers had helped get rid of the evil in Tanah Darah, Fairelle as a whole was not yet safe. And the brothers were still Vampire Slayers. Their abilities had not waned, thought their all-consuming desire to kill vampires had. Which was a comfort. Especially now that Snow was the queen.

Jamen rubbed his hands together in an effort to warm them. The next three months were his turn at Gwyn Manor to take care of the family lands and holding. Being close to the end of December, there wouldn't be much for him to do, but he appreciated the opportunity to have some solitude, to think. There had been so much upheaval in his life in the past years and he'd spent most of it in an alcohol-induced stupor just so he could cope. He'd never anticipated making it through the last two and a half years so he'd never dared to think about anything past getting through the day. But now he could actually look to the future.

Yuletide Festivus was within the week. In Tanah Darah, Snow had taken to decorating for the holiday. But in Gwyn manor there was not a candle, piece of colored glass or garland to be seen. Not that it mattered. Yuletide Festivus was a celebration of light and goodness. A celebration of the people who brought you joy. And he had no one to celebrate with.

His gaze travelled to the emerald ring that bound tightly to his pinky finger. He swallowed hard and wondered where she was right then.

Scarlet had left Westfall after he'd broken it off with her. He'd asked her little sister about her once. She said Scarlet had gone south to stay with family. He'd never dared to track her down. The less people knew of their relationship the better it would be for her. A year later her parents had closed up their shop and moved on as well.

Jamen spotted the small stack of firewood that Erik had left. He piled the logs high in the hearth and placed some kindling underneath. He used a flint and tinder to strike a spark. The tinder caught and licked up the logs. He stared into the flames, letting his mind wander.

Erik had met with the landlord and mayor just a week prior, which meant Jamen had nothing to do other than sleep, eat and possibly ride. He hadn't had time to himself in so long he wasn't sure what he should do first. Perhaps a ride into Westfall to shop for presents for Yuletide. He wouldn't be able to get them to Snow and his brothers for several weeks at least, but it would give him something to do.

A knock on the front door pulled Jamen from the warmth of the fire.

His boots clunked on the wooden floor, echoing through the empty manor as he headed through to the front hall.

The door creaked loudly as he heaved it open. They used the

front door so rarely that it was a wonder it hadn't stuck.

"Good morrow," said a young man said with a smile. "I'm glad I finally caught someone. I've tried for several days to deliver this." The boy thrust a cream colored scroll with a gold seal at Jamen. "Can you see that your Lord gets this?"

Jamen's eye twitched. Though he still wore his travelling clothes there was nothing about his demeanor that should have been read as a servant. He snatched up the scroll and ripped it open.

"That's for—"

"A Lord of Gwyn manor?" asked Jamen. "Yes, you said. I am Lord Jamen Gwyn."

The messenger blanched and stepped back, bowing. "My Lord, I apologize. I was unaware—"

"Forget it." He scanned the parchment. It was a wedding announcement for the son of Sir Malcolm, a friend of Jamen's late father and a bride who's name Jamen didn't recognize. "Who is Lady Greenwater?" Jamen asked, scanning the parchment again.

"She is from down south, from what I've been told, M'lord."

The wedding celebrations were to begin within two days. Jamen sighed. There went his time of solitude.

"Shall I announce your decision M'lord?" the messenger asked.

"I shall arrive on Thursday and stay only the night," Jamen replied.

"Very well, Lord. Again I apologize—"

"None needed." Jamen closed the door, his eyes still on the parchment. The flowing script was in bright blue and adorned with flowers. The announcements he'd commissioned for his own wedding had been very similar.

Breathing deeply he closed his eyes. He'd avoided any kind of celebration in the past three years, as he had nothing to celebrate. It was usually Erik's department to go to these kinds of things. Erik was the eldest and technically the Lord of Westfall. Jamen was only fourth in line. But as Erik had only just returned to Tanah Darah and with the pond that held the portal mirror frozen over, there was no way he would make it in time. Besides, it was only for one night.

He blew out a sigh and rubbed his hands over his face. They'd been locking themselves away from their duties in Westfall for far too long. It was the reason he'd been sent back.

There was no choice. He'd have to go himself.

*****

Scarlet stared in the mirror as her aunt's maid pinned and braided her hair for the pre-wedding celebration. Her red locks were brushed smooth and then woven by Camille's expert hands into an intricate plat.

"Scarlet, dear," said her aunt. "I think the purple dress will be best."

"Yes, Aunt Liza." Scarlet's voice was as flat as her feelings for her soon to be husband.

Her aunt turned. "Scarlet—"

"Sorry," she said. She'd slipped.

Looking at herself in the mirror, she put on the pretty smile Aunt Liza had taught her.

15

"This is what we've hoped and worked for, for the last two years. It's a good match and I'm lucky to have found a rich husband who loves me for my beauty and is willing to overlook my suspicious past."

The mantra that had been drilled into her brain several times a day for the past years.

Her aunt's eyes softened. She laid the dress out on a large pink chair and then walked to Scarlet. Shooing Camille away, she took over Scarlet's hair.

"I understand this is hard for you. I can't begin to know the weight you carry with you in your heart. I've had my heart broken before too of course, but I've never grieved the way you do. After three years, the pain of your loss is still apparent."

Scarlet swallowed the lump in her throat. No matter what she'd done, no matter how hard she'd tried, she couldn't move on. She'd lost her one true love, and in doing so, she'd locked away her desire to love at all. But it didn't matter now. She'd given all that up. Now all she did was put on the pretty smile and hide the pain.

"All that is behind me now," she said.

Her aunt placed a jewel-encrusted comb into her hair. "You'll soon be wed to a handsome man. You'll have all the money you could ever want and with any luck you'll have a child to occupy your time within the year."

Scarlet broke eye contact with her aunt and stared down at the brushes, combs and pins on the vanity. She blinked rapidly, trying to hold back the tears. With Edward, she would have blond babies with peachy skin and bright blue eyes. But what she dreamed about were dark haired, chestnut eyed babies. Two boys and a girl. All with their father's good looks and strength and her smile.

"Scarlet?"

Her aunt's voice pulled her from her thoughts. "Yes, Aunt Liza. Sorry. It must just be last minute nervousness because of the party. I'm fine, truly I am. You've taught me well. Thank you again." She stared at her aunt in the mirror. Aunt Liza's blue eyes crinkled in the corners as she stroked Scarlet's cheek.

"What is our creed, my dear?"

"Love the money, not the man and use everything we have to get both."

"Because..."

"If we do, we get what we want."

"That's right. You already have Edward eating out of the palm of your hand. You just need to forget Jamen Gwyn so that you can keep it that way."

"Of course, Aunt Liza. Water under the bridge."

Her aunt hooked a finger under the chain that dangled at Scarlet's throat and lifted the locket from between Scarlet's breasts.

"Then why not leave this here tonight?"

Scarlet swallowed hard. Her gaze travelled to the small oval shaped locket that hung in front of her nose. Her chest squeezed tight and her stomach clenched. She grabbed the locket and stuffed it inside her chemise.

"Not just yet." Scarlet smiled, but her lips twitched.

17

"Soon he will ask about it."

"Tomorrow," she lied. "I'll take it off tomorrow."

Aunt Liza gave her a knowing frown and shook her head. Then she pulled her shoulders back and Scarlet did the same. They both plastered on their fake smiles and stared at each other.

"You're beautiful, my dear." Her aunt squeezed her shoulders. "Come on now. Let's get you into your dress."

Scarlet nodded and Camille helped her on with her beautiful silken gown. She had a closet full of silken gowns in different colors, all bought for her by Aunt Liza. Everything she had was because of Aunt Liza and now she would be married to a man who would give her the security she needed. She owed Aunt Liza her life. To do anything to shame her aunt would be worse than death.

Aunt Liza headed down to the celebration and Scarlet lingered in the doorway of her room, listening to the sounds of music and talking in the front hall. She dropped her gaze and clutched the locket that dangled between her breasts. Painful memories resurfaced, making a pit grow in her stomach.

She set her shoulders and practiced the "welcomes" and "how do you do's" that Aunt Liza had taught her. She curtsied in her dress, making sure to keep her chin up and her spine straight. All the things she'd never known while growing up the daughter of a lowly shop keep. But the past years had been the crux of her education at Aunt Liza's. That, and how to keep a man happy in bed.

Finally, Scarlet blew out a large breath, pinched her cheeks and closed her door behind her.

Aunt Liza was right of course, Edward was a perfect match for her. Sweet, generous and naïve. With him she would want for nothing. Nothing except for him to be someone he wasn't.

CHAPTER THREE

Jamen pulled his horse up to a large estate on the south edge of the Gwyn lordship. The outside of the estate had been decorated with garlands of mistletoe in reds and greens. The Yuletide Festivus decorations made him warm at the sight. Candles stood all along the drive casting a golden glow over the snow packed ground. After a minute a valet skidded to a halt beside Jamen's steed and took the reigns. Brutin, his horse, reared up and pulled from the valet's grasp.

"Easy." Jamen patted the horse on the neck.

The valet's eyes darted over the length of the horse.

"He's enormous," said the valet. "And not one for strangers, I take it."

He's not the only one. Jamen stared at the stream of people entering the house and swallowed hard. He wanted nothing more than to turn Brutin around and go home. He'd rather face an army of vampires and daemons than the gaggle of geese that entered the party, laughing and chattering. His hands shook as he dismounted.

Jamen handed the reins to the valet. "Be careful with him. And if you have any problems, just let go of the reins and come find me."

The valet nodded.

A manservant stepped up and offered to take Jamen's bag. "Hello Lord, nice to see you again."

It was the boy who'd delivered the invitation.

"I can get it." Jamen untied the satchel and slung it to his back. He removed his sword as well.

The valet and manservant exchanged a look.

"Yes, sir. It's my pleasure. I'm afraid I didn't introduce myself the other day. I'm Fredrick. Please, let me show you to your room."

"Through the back. I don't want to see anyone yet," Jamen said. Still in his riding clothes and snow-soaked cloak, other guests peered at him strangely making the hairs on his neck prickle. He'd hated being stared at.

"Of course." Fredrick bowed again and showed Jamen around the large brick structure to a side entrance.

The kitchen was a bustle of activity. Jamen's stomach growled at the smells of great cooking. Goose and duck, pig and beef were all being prepared. Every vegetable grown in Westfall sat on large platters being dressed for serving.

From the kitchen they travelled up a narrow staircase to the top floor of the house. Fredrick hurried to the third room on the left and opened the double doors. Jamen stared. The grandeur of such a room was beyond the decorations of even his father's manor house. Gold candle holders and a bright silver clock sat on the mantle of a fireplace. Vases full of smelly flowers made his nose itch. The bed was covered in an ivory silk coverlet and more pillows than a person could possibly use.

Every piece of furniture shone and the wooden floor had been polished so much that Jamen feared he might slip. How was he supposed to relax in a room like that?

Fredrick waited as Jamen took everything in.

"Is there a problem M'lord?" he finally asked.

"Uh…" Jamen was at a loss. "Are there possibly any other rooms that aren't so…" He didn't even know how to finish the question without sounding insulting. "Shiny?"

The servant wrung his hands. "Well…Sir Malcolm picked this room out for you especially and—"

"Never mind." Jamen waved his hand. It was only for one night. He just needed to stay long enough to sleep. How many things could he break or dirty before then?

"Shall…shall I help you dress, M'lord?"

"I can do it myself, thank you." Jamen's boots and riding cloak dripped muddy, snowy water. "But perhaps you should hang up my cloak, before I ruin the floor."

Fredrick smiled. "Of course, M'lord."

"And you can stop calling me that. It's just Jamen." He unfastened his cloak and handed it to Fredrick. Then slung his bag off his shoulder and set his sword on the table.

"Of course, M'lord," the servant replied.

"Tell me, Fredrick," Jamen said. "Has everyone arrived yet?"

"Just about, M'lord."

Jamen turned his gaze on Fredrick.

"Jamen," Fredrick corrected himself.

Jamen searched for a place to sit his frozen rear but there was nothing for it, so he gave in and sat on the edge of an immaculate cobalt blue sofa. It had been so long since he'd had a servant, that just letting another man pull off his boots seemed silly now.

Fredrick set his boots by the fire and then hung Jamen's cloak on a hook by the fireplace as well.

Fredrick was young. Younger than even Kellan—.Jamen's chest tightened at the thought of his baby brother.

"Go ahead and tell Sir Malcolm that I have arrived and that I'll be down presently," he said.

"Of course, my—" Fredrick caught himself, smiled and bowed before heading out the door. "Jamen."

When the door closed Jamen leaned forward and rested his forehead in his hands. He should have called for Erik. Just thinking about going down and having to make an appearance at a wedding celebration made him want to tear his own skin off.

All of the petty people going about their lives as if there was nothing in Fairelle to worry about. They were so naïve. So stupid. How could they not believe the truth about the vampires, the werewolves and worse, the other things that had yet to be faced? All around him people fell in love, got married, had parties, and all he'd seen in the last three years was death and decay.

His brother was gone now, like mother and father. Snow was...different, and Flint was still missing. Anger and panic bubbled to the surface. He wanted to yell. To go down and tell all those people to bow to him. To grovel at his feet and to thank him for all he and his brothers had sacrificed to keep them safe, and fat, and oblivious.

Inwardly he cursed himself. Hadn't he been just like them up until a few years ago?

Jamen rose and grabbed his bag. Rummaging around inside he located his flask and pulled off the top. He downed several large swigs before taking a deep breath. Staring at his satchel his eyes lit on a hand-drawn portrait that he was never without. He reached for it and ran his fingers over the faded and smudged parchment. His heart shuddering at the sight.

Beautiful emerald eyes stared at him. Lush, petal pink lips curled into a slight smile. Memories of the feel of those soft lips on his washed over him and settled in his gut.

Jamen tossed the portrait down, closed the bag and took another swig from his flask. He should throw the portrait away, but keeping it was a terrible torture that reminded him of what he'd sacrificed to keep Fairelle safe. No, not Fairelle. Her. He fought to keep *her* safe. Wherever she was.

Jamen pulled on the collar of his jerkin and descended the front staircase to the lower floor. It had been years since he'd been forced to wear his more formal attire. Tight against his throat the jerkin felt like being in a bear hug.

Go in, say hello, wait for the feast, then slip out. That was his plan. He needed to come and represent his family, but that didn't

24

mean he needed to stay the whole night, dancing and talking.

The railings for the stairs were covered in garlands of eldergreens and the house smelled of wassail. The sight and smells made his jaw clench. Memories of his parent's grand parties floated back to him. So much pain. So much loss.

Violins played an upbeat tune in a large room to the left. Guests milled about in the front hall like sheep waiting to be fed.

Upon seeing him, men and women bowed, curtsied and welcomed Jamen with much enthusiasm. They lied, acting like old friends who had missed him. He donned his ritualistic smile and said hello to each person in turn, fighting the urge to curse them out. He knew the whispers behind his back. When you drank and swived as much as he had, word was bound to get out.

He spoke to the Westfall mayor and the mayor's wife and then to the local doctor. Father Ohana, the priest said his hellos, as did the blacksmith.

Jamen stepped into the dancing hall and spotted a banquet table full of finger foods. His stomach growled and he started for the table, the mayor still chattering at his side. He hadn't had a good meal since he'd left Tanah Darah. He'd realized since returning to the empty manor house, just how much he relied on his family.

He filled his small platter with pastries and meat, cheeses and a hunk of bread. He stepped up to grab a cup of mead and was clapped on the back.

"Jamen! Long time no see old friend."

He turned to find Klaus holding the hand of his three year old

25

daughter, Chloe– the spitting image of her mother Belle, his sister Snow's oldest friend.

"Klaus, how are you?" he asked, stuffing an hors d'oeuvre into his mouth.

"My trading business has dropped off a bit, but gambling still pays well." Klaus gave him a toothy grin.

His dirty blond hair had been slicked back into a wavy ponytail. His forest green jerkin and breeches were the nicest thing Jamen had seen Klaus wear. Chloe wore a beautiful pink dress and sported white peonies in her honey colored hair.

Jamen bent down.

"Hello, Chloe." He smiled at her angelic face.

"Hi, Uncle Jamen." She waved. "Daddy got me a bracelet." She held up her hand showing off a dainty gold bracelet.

Business must not be that bad for Klaus.

"It's beautiful. But not quite as beautiful as you are."

Chloe giggled.

"Did you get to dance?" Jamen asked.

Chloe shook her head.

"Well, make sure you save a dance for me, okay?"

She broke into a bright smile and nodded vigorously.

Jamen stood. "Where's Belle?"

Klaus scanned the area, "Ah, here she comes. But Jamen, I need to tell you—"

Belle approached Klaus, but her eyes were on Jamen. She smiled, and her caramel colored eyes brightened for a moment. She looked behind her and then at Jamen again. "Jamen, how are you?" She laid her hand on his arm.

A knot formed in his gut. "I'm well, how are you?" He picked up another piece of food and popped it in his mouth.

She searched his face. "You shouldn't have to be here tonight, why didn't Erik come?"

The knot tightened and he swallowed the food down dry. "He's... he and my other brothers are away. It's fine, I'm fine. I may not like parties, but I think I can manage an hour or two. I'm only staying the night. Maybe tomorrow the four of us can enjoy lunch at the inn."

Something wasn't right. "Jamen, I was trying to tell you—" Klaus began.

A new voice caught Jamen's attention. "Lord Gwyn?"

Jamen turned to find Edward, the groom, striding his direction. A tall golden haired young man his lanky frame moved with grace and precision. He wore a joyful expression.

"Lord Gwyn," he said again, reaching out to shake Jamen's hand. "How wonderful of you to come. I am so glad that you could make my celebration."

The groom. "I'm sorry my elder brothers Erik and Flint could not make it," Jamen said. "They both wish you the best in your up coming marriage. Unfortunately they are out of the area on business. I am Jamen."

"No need to apologize." Edward pumped Jamen's hand up and down and clapped him on the back. "We are grateful you could make it in this chilly weather, Lord Gwyn."

"I'm a poor substitute for my brothers. I'm afraid I'm not too fond of celebrations."

Edward laughed, and envy soured Jamen's stomach at the happiness he exuded. Though Edward was only a year or so younger than Jamen himself, he still held the joy of being in love and blissfully ignorant. At the age of twenty-seven, Jamen felt like he'd seen twice as many years.

"Well, why don't you come meet my bride-to-be," said Edward. "She's a beauty that is sure to make any man want to celebrate."

Belle grabbed onto Jamen's sleeve. "If you don't mind, Edward," she said. "I would appreciate a moment with Lord Gwyn, before he meets your fiancé." Belle curtsied.

Edward looked from Belle to Jamen and back again, his expression perplexed.

"It's all right," said Jamen. He handed his plate to Klaus. "You hold this for me, and Belle, we'll speak after I've said my congratulations." He winked at Chloe. "Besides, I owe a pretty girl a dance."

Chloe smiled and clutched Belle's hand. Jamen's gaze met Belle's again. Her expression tightened. She glanced at Edward before nodding.

"Of course, Lord Gwyn." She curtsied and then backed away to stand next to Klaus.

Jamen followed Edward toward the front of the dancing hall. He looked back to find Belle talking animatedly to Klaus, who shook his head. The pit in Jamen's gut grew.

He wove through the crowd of people standing and watching the dancers spin and twirl across the floor. A group of colorfully dressed women laughed and talked several feet in front of him. The sound of it grated against his eardrums like gravel.

A man stood with two others just in front of the group of women and raised his glass to Edward.

"Lord Gwyn, may I introduce my older brother Lyden and my two friends Mark and Simon," said Edward.

Lynden stuck out his hand. He was almost identical to Edward except that his eyes held a calculating stare. "Lord Gwyn."

Jamen shook without a word.

Lyden sipped his glass as Jamen shook with the other men. When Jamen's gaze met Lyden's again, Lyden smiled.

"Sorry, I've only ever met your older brother Lord Erik Gwyn and you two look nothing alike," said Lyden.

"I get that a lot," Jamen replied. "I resemble Flint more."

Lyden shrugged. "I wouldn't know, I haven't seen a Gwyn in Westfall besides your sister Snow in the past year."

Jamen's fist clenched at his side, his nails biting into his palms. "I didn't know that we were required to make appearances."

Edward gave Lyden an icy look and then smiled at Jamen. "Of course you aren't. You and your brothers are Lords of the area and I am sure you have more pressing things to do than laze about in town like my brother."

Lyden laughed and downed his drink. "True brother. True."

29

Lyden bowed to Jamen and exchanged his empty glass of mead for a full one with a passing servant.

"Please, Lord Gwyn, I promise, my bride is much more amenable than my stuffy older brother." Edward waved him forward and a group of women parted. Edward helped a female from a chair. "Lord Gwyn, may I introduce—"

Jamen heard nothing Edward said after that. His eyes travelled up the violet colored dress to meet emerald green eyes. His heart stopped beating as she locked eyes with him. The smile she had held just moments before disappeared in an instant.

Her hair was the same beautiful color of mahogany wood. Her lush pink lips parted as if she wanted to say something, but then closed again.

The eyes of the surrounding group were upon them. The mayor's rotund wife chatted quickly to the doctor's equally stout spouse.

Jamen chuckled. "I apologize, Edward, you were correct. The beauty of your bride-to-be could bring joy to even the most hardened of men."

He bent forward and lifted her soft slender hand, kissing the back of it. Staring at her beautifully manicured fingernails, he remembered the last time he'd felt her touch.

His heartbeat raced like the hoof beats of his steed as he stood to face her again. Her eyes flashed and her cheeks flushed a beautiful shade of rose.

She broke eye contact and yanked her hand from his grasp.

"You do me too much credit, my Lord," she said. "There are far more beautiful maidens here, for a man such as yourself to be joyed by." She linked her arm in Edward's and gave Jamen a hard stare.

He tried to formulate words, but she left him tongue tied as always. His little Lettie. His Scarlet. The love of his life.

CHAPTER FOUR

Scarlet's heart beat so fast, she thought she might pass out. How could *he* be here? She'd expected Erik, or Flint, possibly Gerall, but not Jamen. Never Jamen. He hated parties.

She tried to gather her wits about her, but his beautiful chocolate eyes were all that she could see. Though they were the same deep pools she'd loved since she was a girl, they'd changed. Hardened and rimmed with shadows, he seemed ages older than the last time she'd seen him.

The stubble he now sported on his jaw, was ruggedly handsome. He'd gained a small scar on his neck, that hadn't been there before. Her fingers twitched to touch him.

"Would you like to dance with her?" Edward asked.

"Excuse me?" Scarlet's gaze whipped up to meet her would-be-husband's.

"A dance, my love. Why don't you dance with Lord Gwyn? Then perhaps we might be able to entice him to actually stay for the feast." Edward smiled at her.

"That's quite all right," said Jamen. His eyes flicked between her and Edward. "I don't need to—"

"I insist," said Edward. "You are Lord over these lands and it's your right to dance with the bride-to-be. It's a good thing we no longer practice the option for you or one of your brothers to spend the first night with her."

Jamen choked and then burst into a fit of coughing.

"Are you all right?" asked Edward. He laughed. "I was kidding of course."

"Of course," Jamen choked out.

A servant stepped up and offered Jamen a drink, which he downed in one large gulp.

When he finished he looked at Scarlet. Please let him say no, she prayed.

"Very well," he said. "But I apologize in advance, my Lady. I'm afraid my dancing skills are a bit rusty."

"Well then, it's time you brush up," said Edward. "Lady Scarlet is a wonderful dancer."

Scarlet's throat felt like she'd eaten ashes from the fireplace. Jamen held his hand out to her. She scanned for Aunt Liza, but couldn't locate her. What was she to do? She hadn't prepared for such a scenario.

Liza's voice sounded in her mind, calming her. "*Play the game, girl. Remember who you are and what you represent.*"

Scarlet beamed up at Edward. "Of course, darling. If I can teach you to dance I'm sure I can teach anyone."

33

Edward laughed and kissed her forehead.

She trembled as she slipped her fingers into Jamen's. His grip was tender but his hands were rough. Not soft like they had been when he'd touched her years before.

Her mind whirled in disbelief as he led her through the crowd and out onto the dance floor. She stood stiff as a board, in the middle of the floor and waited for him to make a move. He stared at her. His eyes drinking her in, long and slow. She cursed her suddenly wobbly knees.

All around people whispered.

"Do something," she hissed through clenched teeth and then smiled.

Jamen blinked rapidly and then cleared his throat. He stepped up to her and the smell of his soap hit her. His arm slipped around the small of her back and his fingers splayed there, drawing her close. Her body tingled and heated at his touch. Damn him for getting a response out of her still.

She stretched out her arm and his fingers closed around hers. He never broke eye contact as he stepped forward and she in turn stepped back.

Their bodies pressed together and moved in perfect unison. The rest of the world blurred and all she could see was him. Her throat clenched at all the things she wanted to say. But she suddenly couldn't remember any of them.

He stared into her eyes and for once she was speechless.

"Hi," he finally said.

34

"Hello." She scanned the gathering and smiled at the houseful of spectators. It was a show and she needed to play her part after all.

"You look beautiful."

Warmth spread over her cheeks to the tips of her ears.

He twirled her around and then brought her back to him. She reminded herself of the last time they'd met and of the hell he'd put her through. She'd promised herself she wouldn't fall for that again, but suddenly in his arms, she was forgetting everything her aunt had taught her.

"How have you been?" he asked.

Play the game. She relaxed into him. "I've been well, thank you. And you?"

His expression saddened. "Surviving."

This couldn't be real. She couldn't really be in his arms again. In a moment she would wake up to find that it had been just one more tantalizing dream of him coming back into her life.

"You changed your surname," he said.

Anger danced over her spine but her smile stayed planted on her lips. She winked at Edward as they twirled past him. "You left me no choice. I was ruined after you rejected me."

"I know. I'm sorry, Scarlet," he whispered.

"I believe you've apologized already." She met his eye and then looked over his shoulder.

"I've missed you."

Her smile faltered. No, Aunt Liza's training had not prepared her for this. The pain in his eyes made her weak. No! She couldn't do this. Not now. Not when she was so close to attaining her goal.

"I am to be wed, my Lord. To Edward. A good man. A man who will make me respectable again and give me a home and children and a life. That's what I want, what I need." She straightened her spine and hardened her gaze. "And he would never leave me."

His face sagged impossibly lower, making her lies taste bitter.

"Of course." His eye took on their signature steely appearance.

"Lord Gwyn," said Edward's father, Malcolm. "May I?" He held out his hand to Scarlet.

"Of course, Sir Malcolm." Jamen let go of her and she stumbled at his quick movement.

Her body chilled at the loss of his warmth. He bowed and kissed her hand once more.

"Lady Scarlet, I thank you for putting up with my clod-footed ways. You are indeed a wonderful dance partner."

Scarlet curtsied. "The honor was all mine, my Lord."

Sir Malcolm took her into his arms and swept her around the floor. Her heart drummed so fast she thought it might expire. She kept her gaze on Jamen as he moved through the crowd until he met up with Belle and together they walked into the front hall.

Scarlet met Sir Malcolm's eye and smiled at him before looking away again and blinking away the tears that threatened to overwhelm her and send her fleeing from the party.

Scarlet picked at her plate, not tasting anything that she put in her mouth. Sir Malcolm asked Jamen to sit by him and the two spoke through the entire meal.

"Is the food not to your liking, my dearest?" asked Edward.

She smiled and set down her fork. "It's wonderful, Edward. I'm afraid that the ride from Aunt Liza's house just tired me out more than I had imagined."

"I can find you something else if you prefer."

Edward's face was kind and his smile bright. He'd been nothing but an eager suitor since they'd first met. Sending her flowers and fruit while she stayed at her Aunt's. On his visits they'd take long walks where she'd listen to him speak of his favorite hobbies and books.

He was a good man, and handsome as well, but for Scarlet, she felt nothing more than a friendship for him. Which was how it was to be of course. Thiers was a business arrangement, nothing more. Not that he knew that.

She lay her hand expertly on his forearm and squeezed. "Thank you for your concern, truly, I'm just a bit tired."

Her gaze travelled over his shoulder to where Jamen watched her like a hawk. Her chest tightened. Taking a deep breath, she swallowed hard. She returned her gaze to Edward, praying Jamen stopped staring at her. If he didn't he was bound to see through her façade sooner or later.

"I hope you feel better." Edward's face held concern. "I would hate for you to be ill on our wedding day. It's supposed to be the most special day of your life. I know it will be for me. Especially our wedding night."

Scarlet's cheeks heated.

"I didn't mean to embarrass you," he said. "It's just… You're so beautiful and I can't wait to make you my wife and spend my time with you in my arms."

She feigned shyness and wondered if he would be surprised by the knowledge she possessed in the arts of lovemaking. Though she'd only been with Jamen that once and no other, her aunt had told her many things and given her even more books to read on the subject.

Almost half of the guests had left already. Only the ones who wanted to impress Sir Malcolm, or Jamen or both, were left.

"I think I'll retire for the evening," she said.

Edward, Sir Malcolm and Jamen stood.

"Are you all right, my dear?" asked Sir Malcolm.

"I'm just a bit tired from the travel and excitement," she replied.

"Of course," said Sir Malcolm.

Aunt Liza's maid, Camille, stepped to Scarlet's side. "Do you need help, M'lady?"

"I am ready to retire for the evening. Would you please let my aunt know?" Scarlet looked for Aunt Liza and noticed for the first time that her aunt's chair at the table wasn't occupied.

"Your aunt has already gone up," said Camille. "She was feeling a bit under the weather herself."

Scarlet looked at Edward. "Goodnight, Edward, Sir Malcolm, Lord Gwyn." She nodded to them in turn. Edward leaned in and gave her a quick peck on the cheek.

"Sleep well, my sweet Scarlet."

Her heart thumped like a rabbit's as Jamen watched her with narrowed eyes. She turned from the group and walked to the first table, thanking the remaining guests for coming.

"I'm afraid I should probably turn in as well. I too am a bit tired from my ride," said Jamen.

Her stomach twisted into a knot and she stiffened. She refused to turn back. Instead she hurried from the room and when she reached the hallway she moved quickly to the stairs in an effort to out run him.

*****

"Of course," said Edward.

"We'll see you in the morning," said Sir. Malcolm.

Jamen nodded and strode to the door. What the hell was he doing? Being near Scarlet was dangerous. Trying to get her alone was even more so. Plus, she was to be married.

She'd changed so much. No more carefree and willful, she was more of a noble woman than he'd ever been a nobleman. Every word she spoke, every lilt of laugher were meant to entice a man and draw him in. It wasn't like her. It wasn't natural.

He hit the stairs just as she reached the top and turned out of sight. He rushed to catch her.

"Scarlet," he called as he reached the top. He turned to make sure no one had heard, but there was no one in the front hall.

Around the lit hallway, candles illuminating every polished

surface. She made no sound as she walked down the sky blue carpet toward her room.

She stopped and Camille the maid turned, but Scarlet didn't.

He wracked his mind for something to say, but he couldn't form words. All he wanted was to feel her in his arms. With her in his arms, he was willing to dance for the rest of his life.

"The celebration was beautiful," he said, walking closer to her. "Were the decorations your doing?"

She turned, her face a mask of society politeness. "I'm afraid not M'lord. Sir Malcolm arranged everything."

"Will you spend Yuletide here then, or go to your parents?"

Her gaze travelled to Camille, who curtsied and continued into a room down the hall. Scarlet waited till Camille was gone. She smiled plainly. "I cannot go to my parents. I am orphaned and live with my Aunt Liza." Her voice was as hollow and rehearsed as his was when he lied about his family.

"I...I'm so sorry, I didn't hear of your—"

Scarlet looked around. "That's the story anyway and I would appreciate it if while you are here Lord Gwyn, if you would please stick to it. I don't need people digging into my past. I've been lucky that so far no one in Westfall has recognized me besides Belle and Klaus. I'd like to keep it that way."

A heavy weight lifted from Jamen's shoulders.

It was a lie to get her a husband. The weight settled down on him again.

"How long has it been since you've seen them?"

She stared at him long and hard before continuing down the hall. "Since I left, almost three years ago."

"And your sister? I know she used to write to you."

She stopped short. "How did you–"

"I asked about you once. She told me that your parents had forbidden her to talk to you, but that she wrote to you anyway."

"She's doing well. She too might marry soon I believe." She walked to a door and turned the handle.

He rushed to her. His blood pumping. She let out a squeak as he lay a hand on her by the arm. She backed into the wall as he moved closer to her.

"Scarlet, I'm sorry. I'm so sorry for everything. I was trying to save you, not hurt you."

He waited for her reply and for a flash he saw his Scarlet. But then her eyes turned cold.

"Save me?"

He nodded. "Yes. Something happened to me. To my brothers. I couldn't explain at the time because it was too dangerous for my family. I was so afraid of you getting hurt that—"

"What happened?" She crossed her arms over her chest, her eyes narrowing.

This was it. The moment he'd waited for all these years. His chance to tell her the truth. "It's hard to explain," he began.

Scarlet glanced both ways down the hall. "No one's here but us, and I have time. I've had three whole years to wait. So come on, explain."

41

Jamen opened his mouth.

She held up her hand. "But whatever you do, don't lie and don't tell me again that you're sorry."

He nodded. He needed to make her understand and forgive him. So that the pain in his soul for what he'd done would finally cease. "Three seasons ago, there was this woman—"

"A woman?" Her voice soured.

Scarlet's face twisted into the beautiful angry pucker that tugged on his heart.

"Yes. A fae woman. At least, I think she was fae. That's not important." He waved his hand. "She came to the manor house."

She cocked an eyebrow. "A fae woman, came to Gwyn Manor?"

"Yes." Jamen bit his tongue to keep from telling her to stop interrupting. "She said there was evil behind the throne of Tanah Darah. That we needed to eradicate the evil before it was too late and all of Fairelle was lost."

"Tanah Darah? The land of the supposed vampires?"

"She did something to us. Magick. I don't know, none of us do. But it was to make us Vampire Slayers. She told us that we needed kill the evil so that the prophecies could be fulfilled. And I was so afraid of marrying you and then you being pregnant and me dying and leaving you penniless with a child. I know it was wrong. It's killed me every day. I know now that my brothers would have looked after you, but I just couldn't do it. I couldn't risk hurting you that way." He stared into her eyes, pleading with her to believe him.

42

He realized that that was the most he'd spoken at one time. His heart felt lighter for having finally told her the truth.

A smile crept across her face and before he knew it, she giggled. Her giggling turned into laughter and Jamen took a step back. The laughter grew louder until she had to cover her mouth with her hand.

"So," she said between laughs. "You are a magical Vampire Slayer." She clutched her sides and laughed some more.

"It…it's true," he stammered.

"A fae woman…came to your house…and poofed you into a Vampire Slayer."

Her laughter pierced him like an arrow.

"She didn't 'poof' us." One moment he'd felt free from the weight of his secret, now it all came crashing back on him ten fold. She didn't believe him. "It's the truth." He clenched his fists at his sides.

Scarlet stopped laughing abruptly. Her gaze met his and the ice from it shot him to the core. "No, Lord Gwyn. Let me tell you what the truth is. The truth is, you took my youth. From the time I was a girl, I wasted my years pining over you. Following you around like a lovesick sow. And you let me. Until one day, you came to my home, reeking of alcohol, and slurred out some apology of how you could not marry me."

"I wanted to come back. For weeks I thought about coming to see you. To make sure you were all right."

"But you didn't. You shut yourself away in your manor house

and refused to see me. Refused to explain. All the while I endured the sad, pitying looks from your brothers who answered the door for the poor shopkeep's daughter. Meanwhile you were spotted in town, at the pub, or the inn, drinking and gambling and cavorting with whores."

Her words were a fresh wound to his heart. How had he been so blind as to think she wouldn't have been hurt so badly?

"I left my home, my parents, my sister, everything and everyone I'd ever known because you didn't want me. And now you stand here, years later, with your lands and your title and you tell me a story about fae and vampires and how sorry you are. Well let me tell you, Jamen Gwyn. I don't care about your apology. You promised me forever and instead you ruined me."

Jamen wished she would strike him. A hit he could handle. Let her scratch his face, beat on his chest, something, anything. Anything other than the words she'd just said. They stared at each other, her eyes like fiery darts.

"I didn't know what forever held at the time."

"Well now my forever is with another man. You need to respect that and let me be."

"Lettie I—"

She lifted her eyes to the ceiling and took a deep breath. When she looked at him again she assumed the position that he'd seen his mother adopt a thousand times when greeting guests she didn't care for but was obligated to be civil to.

"Lord Gwyn, I appreciate you coming to my wedding

44

celebrations. It was a pleasure to see you once again but I ask that in the morning, you get on your horse and go home. As I have wedding and Yuletide Festivus preparations to attend to."

She leaned in and the desire to press his lips to hers made him weak.

"Do not ruin this for me, Jamen. I've worked too hard to get over you and reclaim a position of respectability."

Straightening, her hands clasped in front of her she nodded, dismissing him.

How had he been so ignorant as to think that it wouldn't turn out like this for her? He'd been naïve to think she'd be all right.

"Lady Scarlet." Jamen bowed and turned toward his room.

His limbs moved with a stiffness he'd never experienced before. His chest felt like it had been lined with bricks that were caving in and crushing his heart. His neck heated feeling the burn of her gaze upon him.

Reaching his own room, he opened the door, stepped inside and then closed it. He leaned against it and placed his head in his hands. Tears flowed for the first time in ages.

She hated him. He didn't blame her, he'd ruined her. And not just her, but her family as well. What had he thought would happen? He'd assumed she'd marry, most likely not someone of his position, but well enough. He never expected that she'd have to pretend to be someone else. It would've better to have killed himself than leaving her like that.

A knock sounded on his door and Jamen straightened and

pulled it open. The manservant Fredrick stared at Jamen, his face a mixture of embarrassment and concern.

Jamen blew out a breath and wiped his eyes.

"I came to see if you needed anything before you retire M'lord."

Jamen stared at him for a minute. *Scarlet. I need Scarlet.*

"Drink," he said. "The strongest in the house."

CHAPTER FIVE

Jamen's head pounded. A comforting familiar pain. It helped drown out the hole in his heart. But not by much. He shoved the last of his things into his satchel and retrieved his cloak from where it hung by the dead fire.

He swung the cloak over his shoulders and did the clasp. The only marks of his presence in the overly indulgent bedroom were the three empty bottles on the floor and the blanket someone had pulled from the bed and used to cover him on the couch. Probably Fredrick.

He rubbed his eyes and stepped over to the mirror and washbasin. He poured the water into it and then splashed his face. The cold liquid sent a shock through his system. He splashed it once more before reaching for a towel. His dark curly hair stuck out all over, and though he was tempted to leave it, he was a guest in someone else's home, and representing his family name. As poor an example as he was.

A comb and brush lay on the nearby vanity. Without caring he wet his hair with his hands, ran the brush through it and then set the brush back in its place.

A knock sounded on the door and he grabbed his satchel and sword.

Fredrick stood waiting. "Good afternoon, Lord. I'm afraid I was unable to wake you for breakfast, but if you'd like me to bring you something—"

"That won't be necessary, I'll just take my steed and go. Thank you."

"Of course." Fredrick bowed. "But before you go, master Edward would like to speak with you in the solar."

Jamen didn't want to speak with Edward. Didn't want to see the man that would be taking his Scarlet and making love to her in the near future.

"Where is he?"

"This way." Fredrick waved him down the hall. Jamen's boots punched the wood, the sound reverberating around him and making his head throb.

They passed the room Scarlet stayed in and his eyes lingered on the spot he'd last seen her. His jaw clenched tight. All he wanted was to get home and put his feet up. Now more than ever he craved solitude, and more strong drink.

Camille the maid emerged from the room with a shawl. She looked at Fredrick and her eyes softened and she offered a shy smile and curtsy before continuing down the hallway.

Fredrick looked after her, smiling himself.

"How long have you two known each other?" asked Jamen.

Fredrick's eyes widened. "Oh…uhm…We met when Master Edward started courting Lady Scarlet."

"She likes you."

The young man's cheeks flushed. "Well, I will be most happy myself if she is able to stay on as Lady Scarlet's maid." Fredrick glanced up at Jamen and then at his hands.

They rounded a corner and headed down another wing of the house. Fredrick stopped at the first door and knocked.

"Come."

He opened the door and Jamen stepped into a solar very similar to the upstairs one that his family had used before the death of his mother.

The bright room was a cheery mixture of rich tapestries and warm wood. Soft chairs were scattered about, surrounding several small tables for playing cards. In the far corner Scarlet sat doing needlepoint. Jamen stared, remembering how terrible she'd been at it in her youth.

"I'll never needlepoint when we are wed," she said,

"But I love your bug, bear, tree thingies."

Her jaw dropped in mock offense and she smacked him on the arm. "Thou offendest me, sire!"

"Do I now?" Jamen tackled her to the grass, her auburn hair fanning out around her beautiful face. Dipping his head he caught her lips with his. The taste of strawberries and cream lingered in her mouth as their tongues dances together.

"My Lord?"

Jamen broke his gaze and turned to where Edward, Sir Malcolm, Lyden, and Edward's two friends, that sat playing cards. He strode to them and nodded.

"Forgive me. I'm not quite awake yet, I fear," he said.

"Not at all, sit." Sir Malcolm pulled out a chair. "Lord Gwyn, this is my eldest son Lyden and Edward's friends–"

"Yes we met last night." Jamen shook Lyden's hand and then the hands of Simon and Mark.

Sir Malcolm, Lyden and Edward were all the spitting images of each other at different stages of life. With their light hair and eyes and boyish smiles it was easy to see why Scarlet would be attracted to Edward. His easy demeanor was nothing like Jamen's.

"I'm afraid I must be getting back to Gwyn Manor." Jamen's gaze wandered to the corner where Scarlet studied her needlepoint.

"But the ride is long and the wedding is only yet a few days off. Surely you can stay until then," said Sir Malcolm.

"We are all going hunting tomorrow night. We're to bring back a stag for the wedding feast. You must come with us," said Edward.

The other men at the table nodded.

"Thank you but, I'm afraid I'm not much of a hunter."

Edward laughed. "Well, if you are not much of a hunter, the way you are not much of a dancer, then you are better than the rest of us."

"Come," said Lyden. "What we lack in hunting skills we make up for in company." Lyden looked at Jamen with the same intensity that he had the night before. Something about the man didn't sit right with him. He made a note to ask his brothers about Lyden.

It was Jamen's duty to represent Erik and their family. Erik would accept, go, have fun and make sure Edward and Sir Malcolm were appeased. But Jamen wasn't Erik.

"Thank you again, but I really should be going. I'll return on the morning of the wedding to help you celebrate." Jamen nodded and turned.

"Please, Lord Gwyn," Edward said.

"Jamen." He turned and held up his hand. "It's just Jamen. And I really need to get home. I had only just returned home when I got the announcement."

"Surely a few more days won't make a difference." Edward turned and called over his shoulder. "Lady Scarlet, ask him to stay."

Jamen froze on the spot.

Edward strode to Scarlet and led her by the hand toward Jamen. Her eyes held anguish as she stopped a few feet away.

"Wouldn't it be wonderful if Lord— Jamen, helped bring down the stag for our wedding feast? It would surely mean good fortune to all those at the celebration."

Scarlet peered at Jamen. "It would."

"Ask him, my bride. Ask him to stay." Edward smiled down at Scarlet, who kept her gaze trained on Jamen. It bothered Jamen to see Scarlet being used as a pretty pawn.

His soul felt cleaved in two. Part of him wanted her to ask him to stay. The other part hoped she cursed him and told him to leave, as she had the night before.

"It would bring us great happiness if you would stay." Her voice was kind but her eyes were emotionless.

"Come now," said Edward. "With such a beauty asking, how can you possibly say no?"

Jamen stayed silent for a moment. Such beauty indeed. Scarlet was unparalleled. Her silken red hair and peach skin highlighted her blossom colored lips and sparkling–

"I fear you will have quite a time of it in the future, Edward," he replied.

All the men in the room burst into laughter. Scarlet's face flushed a beautiful shade of rose and her eyes narrowed on him. Embarrassing her had not been his intention.

Edward let go of her hand and clapped Jamen on the shoulder. "Wonderful. It's settled then. We shall leave tomorrow, weather permitting, and find a stag for the wedding feast. Now, let us play cards while we bask in the glow of the Yuletide candles and drink wassail till we can stand no more." Edward motioned to a maid and butler who brought over a tray of spice cakes and cups of wassail for everyone.

Sir Malcolm motioned to the seat next to him and Jamen removed his traveling cloak and handed it to Fredrick along with his bag and sword. He sat silently in the chair, while Lyden dealt a new hand.

"Do you always carry a sword with you?" asked Lyden.

"For the most part."

"You must live a dangerous life," Lyden laughed.

52

Jamen met his gaze. "You have no idea."

Despite his anxiousness, the smells and tastes reminded him of better days at Gwyn Manor. Days when Yuletide Festivus was shared with his family and friends. With songs and joy and laughter. It tore at him knowing that when he returned home there would be no one and nothing there for him but the walls and the stone.

Scarlet asked him to stay. Damn her for doing it. And damn him for wanting to.

*****

Scarlet knocked on the door to her aunt's room. She hadn't seen Aunt Liza since the day before. Liza had come down with an upset stomach and was confined to bed.

"Come in," Camille called.

Scarlet pushed open the door. The curtains had been drawn. Only the soft glow from the candlelight lit the area of the bed.

"Come in, my dear." Her aunt sat up.

Scarlet walked to the bedside and pulled up a chair. Her aunt's beautiful silver hair stuck out from her braid in all directions. Her waxen skin held a sheen of sweat.

"How are you, Aunt Liza?"

Her aunt smiled. "A bit tired and my stomach won't keep much down except the tea Camille brings me. But don't worry."

"Maybe I should fetch the doctor."

Liza waved her off. "Oh, pishtosh, I'll be fine by tomorrow I'm sure. How go the celebrations?"

Scarlet looked down at her hands. *How did the celebrations go?*

Edward was wonderful, attentive and sweet. She played the part of enamored wife to be. The man she'd who'd broken her heart stayed just down the hall from her, testing her resolve every minute as she tried to keep away from him. And on top of it all, she was being forced to needlepoint.

"The decorations and food have been amazing," she said. "Sir Malcolm surely has many connections to be able to procure such beautiful things. Festivus has always been my favorite holiday and since you took me in, I've had much to be grateful for."

Her aunt's eyes narrowed and her lips twisted into a slight smile. "That's not what I asked. Is there a problem with Edward?"

"No."

Her aunt's expression told her that she'd answered too quickly. Scarlet smiled and calmed herself before speaking again. "No. Everything with Edward is just perfect."

"Good girl." Her aunt nodded. "I heard a Gwyn Lord has arrived. How is Erik?"

Scarlet swallowed hard. "Erik couldn't make it. He and several of the brothers are travelling apparently."

"So Flint Gwyn came then? He's quite a brooder from what I remember of him."

Scarlet glanced down at her trembling hands.

"Scarlet, look at me girl."

Scarlet met her aunt's gaze. She swallowed hard and willed her aunt not to ask.

"It's not Flint either, is it?"

Scarlet shook her head.

Her aunt let out a sigh and rubbed her face with her hands. "From the look on your face I assume it won't be Gerall. So, have you spoken to *him*?"

"Yes." Scarlet cleared her throat and spoke again. "Edward insisted that we dance last night, as was Jamen's right as the representing Lord of the area..."

"Scarlet." Her aunt's voice was a warning.

"I've done nothing to show interest. We danced and he seemed as uncomfortable by it as I. Last night I told him I loved Edward and that he should leave as soon as possible." It wasn't exactly the truth. She'd not told him she loved Edward. That was one lie she would not utter.

"It's not you *showing* the interest that worries me. Remember what he did to you. How he dropped you without so much as a word of explanation. You can't let yourself be pulled in by his charms again. We've worked too hard. I've worked to hard—"

Scarlet clutched her aunt's hand. "I know and I'm so grateful to you for all you've done. I'm not going to let Jamen Gwyn back in. I won't let him get to me. He ruined me and I can never forgive him for that... and for other things."

Liza's eyes softened. "I'm sorry, child. That's not what I meant. All I'm trying to say is... I was there with you, through the worst of it. I saw what you went through and I don't want to see you hurt again."

"Thank you Aunt Liza."

"When does he leave?"

"Edward has requested he stay till the wedding."

"Then do everything in your power to avoid him. Give him no reason to think that you still carry a spark for him."

"I don't—"

Her aunt held up her hand. "You think you don't, but a part of you always will whether you admit it or not. Don't be so naïve. The moment you don't acknowledge your emotions—"

"You become a slave to them. I understand." She nodded. She understood, all too well the cost of starting over. A cost that would haunt her forever she feared.

Scarlet patted the locket that hid beneath her bodice.

"Keep close to Edward and don't give him reason to doubt your affections. In a few days Jamen will return to Gwyn Manor and you will begin your new life."

"Of course." Scarlet smiled.

"You must not allow him another chance. If you do, all of my wealth and friendships won't be able to save you again."

Scarlet nodded to her aunt and clutched her locket tight in her fist. If she messed up again, no one in all of Fairelle could save her.

CHAPTER SIX

Scarlet walked the grounds of the estate wrapped tightly in a cloak to keep out the chill. Her mind revisited every moment with Jamen from the first time she'd met him, to the present. She clutched her locket tight and attempted to formulate a plan.

Jamen would be leaving with Edward and the others in the morning. She just needed to avoid him until then. After they returned she would be so busy with the wedding preparations that there would be no need to worry. And under no circumstances could she allow herself to be alone with him.

Scarlet found herself at the door to Sir Malcolm's stable. The smell of fresh hay and leather made her smile. It had been a long time since she'd had a horse of her own. Her horse had been the first privilege her parents had taken away after–. Thoughts of her parents made her frown.

Memories of walking with her small bag, the miles and miles to her aunt's house in the south, replayed in her mind. The blisters on her feet. The ache of her body. The scar she still bore on her ankle where she'd tripped on a rock and gashed herself. Then the anger in her aunt's eyes when she'd seen Scarlet's state.

The cursing Aunt Liza had done when she found out what had happened to Scarlet was more than even Scarlet had done.

Scarlet sighed. It didn't matter now. Those nightmares were in the past.

She pulled open the door and stepped inside the stable. Light filtered through the ceiling and illuminated streaks across the hay lined floor. The sounds of whinnying and pawing lightened her heart. She missed her horse Annabelle.

Hitching up her gown she walked from stall to stall. The horses stood with their heads out, waiting to be pet. She rubbed each nose in turn, speaking to the horses. The first thing she would ask Edward for was a horse. Perhaps he'd even go riding with her. Not the way she used to ride. Free and unbidden by the conventions of society. Wearing pants, not a dress. The wind in her hair, the sun on her face. But still ride, she'd be able to ride. Maybe he'd even take her in the woods to hunt. She'd pretend she didn't know how and let him feel like a hero for having taught her. The idea of happiness with Edward struck her for the first time.

Scarlet reached the end stall and her eyes widened. An enormous black steed hung in the back. He stood close to six feet at the withers. His midnight colored eyes stared at her. She'd never seen such a steed.

"Hey, big fella," she cooed.

He pawed at the ground and snorted.

"It's all right." She glanced around and found a bundle of carrots sitting on a hay bale nearby. She took one and held it out to him.

"Come on, boy. I won't hurt you."

"His name is Brutin."

Scarlet dropped the carrot and backed up. Jamen sauntered over and picked up the carrot. Her heart fluttered like a butterfly's wings. So much for the plan not to be alone with him. She needed to leave.

Jamen walked to the stall and opened the door.

The horse moved to him and pressed his nose into Jamen's shoulder.

"Do you want to feed him?"

"I… Yes. I do." Damn her love of horses and the joy they brought her.

Jamen held the carrot out to her and she took it.

The animal seemed even more enormous, looming above her. "What happened to Fallon?" she asked.

"I still have him, but Brutin has also been mine for a couple of years now."

She stared up into the horse's deep eyes and a trickle of fear skittered through her. "He's the largest animal I've ever seen."

Jamen laughed. "He's pretty big. Flint's horse Ripper is larger though."

She narrowed her gaze on Jamen and he smiled.

"I'm not lying."

Scarlet swallowed hard at the sight of his smile. It had always been a rare commodity. And the sight of it still warmed her in places she didn't want to think about.

He scanned the stalls. "Where's Annabelle?"

"My parents wouldn't let me—" She stopped short. "I didn't take her when I left for my aunt's. I needed to leave everything from my old life behind."

Jamen's brows furrowed. "You took nothing?"

"Only a few small things that I packed in a satchel." The twitching of his fingers caught her attention and she stifled a smile. She caught his eye again. "What are you drawing?"

"What?"

She pointed to his fingers. "Your fingers are drawing something on your pant leg. You always used to do that."

He looked down at his hand and rubbed his fingers together. "I didn't even know I was doing it."

She couldn't stand to see his pained expression when he looked up.

"Stop staring at me like that." She pushed her hair off her shoulder.

"Like what?"

"Like you want to apologize again."

"I won't."

"Good. Apologies are wasted unless they get you what you want."

His brows furrowed again. "Why would you say that?"

She shrugged. "Because it's the truth."

"According to who?"

Scarlet licked her lips. He knew her too well. The mantras her aunt had taught her were not something he would buy.

Jamen held out his hand to her. "Come here."

"Why?"

"You said you wanted to feed him." Jamen jerked his thumb toward the horse.

She stared at his outstretched hand for a moment and then stepped next to him. He pushed her in front of Brutin and wrapped his arms around her from behind. The sensation made her hands tremble.

"Here," he whispered in her ear. He lifted her hand in his own and extended the carrot to Brutin. The horse sniffed it for a second before taking it with his lips.

Scarlet laughed. Her heart soared at the triumph.

"You still have the touch." Jamen's warm breath caused her neck to prickle with goosebumps. She closed her eyes and swallowed, hoping to feel the brush of his lips on her neck. Brutin pushed against her palm with his nose and she opened her eyes again. She stepped out of Jamen's grasp and ran her fingers up over Brutin's ears to his soft mane.

"He's amazing," she whispered.

"He likes you." Jamen backed away. "He doesn't usually warm up to other people."

She glanced over, "Sounds like his owner."

"And how is that?" Jamen crossed his arms over his chest and leaned against the wall.

61

"Are you joking?" She laughed, making his frown lines deepen. "Jamen Gwyn, growing up the only friend you made was Klaus and that was only because no one else would be friends with him."

He shrugged. "I had my brothers and Snow, I didn't need anyone else."

"It took you four years before you even spoke to me more than just to say hello."

"Maybe I'm shy."

She snorted and shook her head. "Don't try to lie to me, I know you too well."

His eyes grew serious. "Yes, you do."

A flutter stirred her insides to melted butter. She looked away. "Don't look at me like that."

"Like what this time?"

"You know, like what."

He stepped closer and she sucked in a breath. Their eyes locked and her heart pounded. She couldn't let this happen, couldn't let him in. She needed to remember her duty to her aunt.

He picked up the locket that had escaped her dress.

"You kept it." He ran his thumb over the golden inlayed surface that bore her initials.

Her blood pumped so hard she could hear it in her ears.

"Don't touch that." She snatched it away and shoved it in her bodice.

"Why? I gave it to you."

Anger heated her belly. "Yes, you did and it's mine."

He laughed lightly.

She clenched her jaw until it hurt. "What's so funny?"

He stared at her hard for a moment. "There you are. I knew you were in there somewhere."

He moved his hand up to her face and caressed her cheek but she slapped it away, making him chuckle again. She let out an exasperated grunt and stamped her foot, which made him really laugh.

"You son of—"

"Why, Lady Scarlet? What would Edward say to hear you speaking like that?"

Scarlet stopped herself from spewing forth the string of profanity that lay on her lips. She'd learned the bad habit of swearing from Jamen and Klaus. A habit she was still trying to break.

He reached out and grabbed her face in both palms. She couldn't make words form.

She rubbed her cheek into his hand. The rough calluses sparked waves of pleasure that rippled through her like a tidal wave and settled between her thighs.

His laughter stopped and he stared into her, making her legs feel like jelly. He stroked her cheek with his thumb.

"I see you, Scarlet Mason," he said.

In that moment all the walls she'd built crumbled to dust. Once more she felt like herself. The "her" that only he knew. Only he would ever know.

Her chin quivered. She wanted his arms around her so much it made every muscle in her body hurt.

"I see you, Jamen Gwyn," she whispered.

"Scarlet?"

She pulled from Jamen's touch.

Edward, Lyden and his friends entered the stable and headed for them.

"What are you doing?" Edward asked.

*****

Jamen dropped his hands from Scarlet, his heart aching to feel her skin again.

Edward's face was jovial, but his eyes darted from Jamen to Scarlet. He stepped up and put his arm around her waist possessively, the scent of alcohol wafting off him. The move made Jamen want to rip Edward's arm from its socket.

Lyden moved next to his brother, his eyes scanning the scene.

"Lady Scarlet was just admiring my steed and wishing me luck on bringing back a stag for your celebration," Jamen said. "She said she'd like for us to keep the antlers for her if possible."

Edward looked at him for a minute before laughing. "What would a you want with antlers, my sweet?"

Both he and Edward stared at Scarlet. Jamen had put her on the spot. *Again.* He just couldn't get it right.

"Well...I..." She smiled. "If you must know, I was going to have them mounted for you. As a present."

"Why would we want such a thing hanging in our room?"

64

Scarlet's face flushed and glared at Jamen then laid her hand on Edward's chest. "Of course," she said. "You're right, darling. It was a silly idea. Feel free to do with them as you wish."

Anger rushed through him like a heat wave him. Scarlet never would have let him get away with making a decision like that. She would have fought him for what she wanted until he gave in. Submissive Scarlet made bile rise in his throat.

"If you will excuse me," she said. "I think you've had a bit more to drink than I'm used to and I need to go see to my aunt."

"Is she still not well?" Jamen asked.

"No, my Lord. I'm afraid she is not." She moved from Edward's grip and curtsied to both Edward and Jamen before exiting the stable.

Edward watched her go and Jamen watched Edward. All he exuded was love for Scarlet, which made Jamen dislike him all the more.

Stop this already! Dammit, man, she isn't yours anymore and never can be as long as there are beasts in the world hell bent on killing all humans.

"I can't wait to get her into my bed," said Edward turning to Jamen. He swayed slightly and bumped into his friends, who snickered.

"She is quite the loveliest of creatures. Don't you agree, Jamen?" asked Lyden.

Jamen's fist closed so tight he was afraid he might break his own fingers. "Indeed she is."

"I'm glad I found her before any other men in the area had a chance," said Edward. "Her beauty is quite exquisite. I'm sure if I'd waited even a week more to ask for her hand, I've had to fight off a dozen other suitors."

"She's one of a kind." Jamen's throat constricted and he tried to clear the lump.

"From her appearance and demeanor you'd never know that she isn't legitimately a Lady. Her aunt took her in to save her reputation. Scarlet was engaged once before, you see. He dropped her. Rumor has it that it was because she wasn't pure. I don't care about that though. And everyone knows the rumors about her Aunt Liza and how she amassed such a large fortune."

"No," said Jamen through a clenched jaw. "What do people say?"

Edward continued without noticing. "Word is that she was just as beautiful as Scarlet in her day. Men threw themselves at her, offering huge sums for just for one night in her arms." He laughed. "Even if Lady Scarlet is a virgin though, I will happily take the time to train her, if it means a few more hours with her body nuzzled close to mine."

Blood pounded in Jamen's ears, so deafeningly loud, that he wondered how he hadn't burst something vital.

He was halfway sure that Edward's words were meant as a compliment to Scarlet, but it was hard to tell. If he'd been anywhere else he would have beaten Edward unconscious by now. His fingers itched to feel the steel of his sword. To hear the rattle of Edward's breath as he sucked in air one last time.

Edward's brother and friends laughed and then moved on to saddle their mounts. He clapped Jamen on the shoulder. Jamen's fist rose in reflex, but he tucked it into his armpit and crossed his arms. He needed to get out of there. He wasn't sure how much longer he'd be able to control his temper.

"You like your women more experienced, don't you, Lord Gwyn?" At the closer proximity the smell of liquor wafted off Edward like the stink of a skunk. He wondered if this was how he'd appeared to Scarlet and her father that awful night three years prior.

Jamen gritted his teeth and rolled his shoulder. Edward removed his hand.

"You know. I think that I am not feeling up to hunting after all. I believe that perhaps you and your father and friends should go without me tomorrow."

Edward bowed. "I've offended you. I apologize. I didn't mean to insinuate—"

"It is true. I have spent many a night in the arms of experienced women. A fact that I am not proud of. But when a man loses his one reason for living, he sometimes finds himself weak in front of temptation."

Edward's face paled. "My Lord, I am truly sorry and didn't mean to offend."

Jamen nodded. "I'm sure you didn't. If you will excuse me, I'll let you get to your afternoon ride." He turned on his heel and closed Brutin's stall closed before storming out of the stable.

He stomped across the yard, his boots crunching on the gravel, his breath puffing out in white clouds. There was no way he could spend the night in the woods tomorrow listening to Edward moon over Scarlet.

Scarlet should've been his, would have been his. Had it not been for the Slayer calling they would be happily married and at Gwyn Manor with a couple of babies to chase after. Instead, he had to listen to another man's plans to bed her.

Why had they been chosen? Why had it been made his family's responsibility to keep Fairelle safe?

His shoulders sagged and he paused before continuing on. What did it matter why? What was done was done. And in the end, how could he judge? He wasn't better than Edward.

How many a night had he spent in the arms of a woman he'd paid for? How many fights? How many drunken stupors, being dragged home by Flint or Erik, only to be tended to by Snow? All in an effort to diminish the pain and forget.

The familiar, constricting pain settled in his chest, made his ribs ache. He couldn't change the past but he could let her have a future, like he'd planned for her when he'd broken it off. Edward was good and decent enough, when he wasn't drinking, which Jamen had a feeling he didn't do often. That alone made him a stronger man.

Edward's father was wealthy and they could provide for her. Jamen's gaze travelled over the estate. She would be happy here surrounded by children. Back at Gwyn Manor they didn't even have servants anymore.

Images of Scarlet, laying underneath him, flashed into his mind. Her creamy skin, her soft caress, her lips. The emotion in her eyes as they'd made love, just that one time, the night before his life had changed forever. His heart sank.

Of all the terrible things he'd done in his life, leaving her was the one he regretted the most. Gods help him, it wasn't the killings, the fights, the drinking, gambling and whoring. It was leaving her.

CHAPTER SEVEN

Edward, Lyden, and his friends took off for a ride. Jamen didn't know where they were going and he cared even less. He needed help. He needed Snow and his brothers. He hadn't realized how much he relied on them till Scarlet had reminded him of his lack of friends growing up.

Erik and Gerall were the sensible and logical ones. Hass and Ian kept things fun. Flint knew exactly how he felt about everything, and Snow... Snow's love kept them all together. He hadn't needed anyone outside his family till he'd met Scarlet.

He remembered the first time he'd seen her in her father's shop. A teen, her thick, shiny mahogany hair had hung almost to her waist. She'd worn a dress the color of poppies and her hair had been adorned with baby's breath. He'd tried to play her off as nothing but a girl, but Klaus had seen right through his lie.

Jamen had gone into Westfall everyday after that for a month, just to catch a glimpse of her. Sometimes she saw him and smiled. Other times he'd just watch her from afar while she helped her

70

parents, or braided her little sister's hair and then played dolls near the village fountain. Several times he'd even sketched her when he'd gotten home. Drawing her eyes, her smile her hair until it was perfect.

She'd been happy, stubborn and carefree then. So different than the woman he'd turned her into by leaving. The darkness of guilt shrouded his thought and he turned from the window in his room to look for his bag. He rummaged inside for his flask. Tipping it to his mouth, he waited for the burn of the alcohol to numb his anguish. But the liquid was gone.

Damn!

Throwing down the flask he stormed into the hallway. Taking the back stairs to the kitchen.

"Were you paid this week?"

Jamen slowed his steps just outside the kitchen.

"No. Master Lyden said that he would make sure we were paid after the wedding," said a female.

"I bet we won't. I overheard Master Lyden and Sir Malcolm in the solar. This wedding is costing a fortune. He spared no expense," said another.

"Including our pay." The first woman snorted.

Surely Sir Malcolm wasn't penniless. Perhaps he was just holding their pay to insure they did their best for the wedding celebration.

"Sir Malcolm said he is expecting a large sum of money to come in after the wedding, but I'm already looking for a new place of employment. It's a bad time of year to be out of work. I'd rather know I have somewhere to go if it comes to it. If I wanted to work for free, I'd stay at home."

All of the women laughed.

Jamen stepped through the door. Three women had their backs to him, peeling potatoes. Fredrick and Camille sat by the fire tending to a kettle, their heads close together.

"Maybe I should look as well," said the cook. "I wonder if the bakery is hiring. I know the baker just died and his daughter is now running things."

"I didn't know he had a daughter," said a maid.

Fredrick pulled the kettle from the hook and turned. "Lord Gwyn." He set a kettle and tea cup on a tray and wiped his hands on his breeches. "Can I help you, sir?"

Everyone in the kitchen turned abruptly. Their faces betraying their obvious distress.

"I need a drink," he said.

"Of course." Fredrick bowed. "Should I fetch some water?"

"Stronger." He rubbed his temples at the memories of his arms wrapped around Scarlet in the stable.

Fredrick nodded and scurried off to the pantry. He returned moments later with two large bottles, reminiscent of the ones he'd brought on the first night.

Jamen grabbed them. "Thank you."

"Of course. I just need to help get this tea and food up to Lady Eliza and then I can stop by to see if you need anything else."

"This will suffice." Jamen headed back up the stairs. When he got to his room he threw open the door and stepped inside. He hadn't even made it to the small couch before he uncorked a bottle and drank until it was half gone. He gasped for a fiery breath as the burn stung his throat and warmed his gullet. Reaching into his satchel he pulled out the portrait of Scarlet and traced her lips with his thumb.

He should leave as he said he would. His family name be damned he should return to Gwyn Manor and forget the wedding. He rubbed the parchment between his fingers imagining the feel of her velvety cheek. Anger bubbled within him and he stood suddenly and flung the bottle at the fireplace. It shattered onto the logs. Steam sizzled from the wood sending a sweet burnt smell through the room.

He couldn't do this. There was no chance for them. He was a Slayer, she was a woman without an ounce of an idea as to what waited out there for them. Vampires, Demons, Werewolves, Dragons.

He needed to crush the budding hope he held onto like a bug. There was no place in Fairelle where she would be safe if she were at his side.

*****

Scarlet ate dinner with Edward, his father, Lyden and friends after the men returned from their daily ride. From the smell of his breath in the stable she was surprised none of them had fallen off their horses and hurt themselves. She prayed that drinking wasn't a habit Edward partook in regularly.

There was no sign of Jamen. Sir Malcolm held dinner waiting for him until Fredrick informed them that Jamen had some things to attend to and to eat without him.

Her insides churned with a soup of relief and nervousness, but the announcement made Edward especially quiet.

Aunt Liza showed no signs of getting better. When she'd gone to visit earlier her aunt had barely been able to sit up. The slightest of movements caused her aunt severe cramping and nausea. Scarlet had sat and read to her aunt till called for supper.

Scarlet sat silently with the men, listening to them speak of their upcoming hunt and caught a glimpse of what her new life would hold, as the only female. With the men talking about business or hunting or cards. No one asking her about her needlepoint or her flower arrangements or how she spent the rest of her day keeping busy. Not that she'd want to talk about the most mundane existence anyway. If she was lucky she would have babies to play with and teach; the cook to tell what to prepare and the maids to oversee. Parties to plan and events to attend. She touched her locket. *If* she were lucky.

"We'll head to the far eastern end of Westfall and then north to the border of Wolvenglen Forest," said Sir Malcolm.

"Isn't that dangerous?" she asked.

"Only for those who are inexperienced hunters, my dear." Edward patted her hand.

For the first time in years she doubted the course her aunt had taught her. The course of using men to get what she wanted.

Especially since she wasn't getting the one she truly wanted. Flowers and overseeing maids and listening to men talk was not her idea of a fulfilled life. Her idea was being free to do what she wanted, go where she wanted, without being treated like a pretty doll. Being able to ride her horse, or hunt, or play cards and games or any of the myriad of things she used to love to do, before Aunt Liza's tutoring.

Her parents had taught her to follow her heart, but that wasn't so in higher classed society. Here in the world of, Yes, dear and No, dear and I'll sit here and needlepoint till my fingers bleed, dear, nothing was as she wanted it. She wasn't herself. It hadn't been that way with Jamen.

When they had been together they'd taken long rides through Westfall. Picnicked by the lake. Spent time with Snow and Belle and Klaus, playing cards and telling stories. When he wasn't helping out around Gwyn Manor and she wasn't helping her parents at the shop, they were out doing what they wanted. It hadn't mattered what they'd done, so long as they were together.

Her chest squeezed at the thought of him. Was he really attending to business or was it something else keeping him from dinner? She hoped he wasn't becoming ill.

"Something on your mind Scarlet?" Edward's voice broke through her revere.

"I'm sorry?" Her skin warmed as she realized every eye was upon her.

"I asked what you were thinking. You laughed."

"I did? I didn't realize." She grasped for something to say.

"Leave her alone, Edward. It isn't good to know all of a Lady's thoughts. If we did, we'd never be able to stay married," Sir Malcolm boomed. All the men broke out into raucous laughter.

Scarlet laughed along side them, her fingers gripped tight under the table.

"Sweet Lady," Sir Malcolm said. "I mean no offense, of course. I am simply saying that you have a right to your own thoughts is all."

"Thank you, Sir Malcolm. I am sure it would be the same if a wife was to hear all of her husband's thoughts." She gave Edward a rueful smile and winked at him.

Sir Malcolm nodded his silver head and lifted his glass. "Tis true. A toast. To the secrets we keep. May they never come to light."

The group toasted together and Scarlet drank her mead in one gulp.

"And with that, if you gentlemen will excuse me," she said. "I will be off to check on my aunt."

"Again you haven't eaten," said Edward.

She glanced at her plate. "That is because I am saving myself so I may feast on the stag you bring back without worrying about my figure on our wedding day."

Edward lifted her hand and kissed the back of it. "Whether svelte or curvy, you will always be the most beautiful creature in Fairelle."

"I hope you still feel that way after several babies have rounded my hips," she quipped.

Scarlet stood and the men did as well. She curtsied and said her goodnights and then stepped into the hall. Fredrick stood by the front door. She approached him with a heavy stride.

"Is Lord Gwyn really attending to business?" she asked.

Fredrick's brow furrowed and his eyes shot toward the dining room. "No, M'lady."

She rubbed her clammy hands together. "Is he ill?"

"Well...he's—"

She didn't let him finish. Striding up the stairs she made for Jamen's room. She rapped on his door. "My Lord? Lord Gwyn, are you all right?"

A moan and a crash sounded from inside. She jumped and pushed open the door. Jamen lay on the small couch, covered in a blanket. He moaned again and rolled over. Her stomach lurched. He *was* ill.

She closed the door behind herself and rushed to his side, feeling his forehead.

"Jamen, can you hear me?"

He tossed and moaned but said nothing.

"Please, Jamen, say something."

"Lettie," he mumbled. He turned toward her, a piece of parchment clutched in his hand. His bloodshot eyes opened and he blinked several times. "Lettie."

The smell of alcohol turned her stomach.

She frowned and stood. An empty bottle lay on the floor near the table, another had broken by the fire.

Anger whipped through her. "You're drunk," she spat.

He tried to focus on her. He sat up and rubbed his messy hair with his hands.

Memories of him stumbling through her house to apologize began to plague her.

"How could you, Jamen? Here, in Sir Malcolm' home. How could you dishonor yourself, your family?"

His gaze intensified. "Dishonor? You have no clue what I have done to bring honor to my family," he slurred.

"And you think getting drunk is honorable? Do you know the whispers around Westfall? About you, about your brothers?"

Jamen got to his feet quicker than she could have thought possible and swayed only slightly.

"What rumors?" he demanded.

His body loomed close to hers. His tan tunic lay open, exposing a fine swirl of dark curls on his chest. A puckered pink scar ran from his sternum to his collarbone. Where had he gotten that? His gaze made her breath quicken. The air suffocated her.

"Nothing. Go to bed." She turned to leave but he grabbed her arm.

"What rumors?"

A tremor of fear and excitement rippled through her.

"Tell me!"

"You're hurting me, Jamen. Let go." She wrenched free of him. He grabbed at her again but she pushed him hard in the chest. "Don't touch me, you drunken toth."

He stumbled into the couch and sat down heavily. A smile spread across his face.

"What?" she huffed.

"You." He shook his head. "You'd never speak this way to Edward would you? But me? I can't even get drunk without you telling me off. Why is that? Why won't you let Edward see the real you? The girl who loves to drink ale and swear and play cards? The girl who rides bareback across Westfall and swims in the ponds with nothing on but her bloomers."

She opened and closed her mouth several times. Because with Jamen she could be herself. Because with him she had nothing to lose.

She moved close and leaned over him till their eyes locked.

"Because I care about *his* opinion." She regretted it in an instant. If she had struck him physically she didn't think he could've looked more hurt.

His lips drew into a grim line and he nodded. "Goodnight, Lady Scarlet. Thank you for coming to see that I was still breathing." He stood and pushed past her.

"Jamen I'm sorry, I didn't—" She reached for him but he stepped out of her grasp. She clutched her hands over her breasts.

"No. You're right. Edward is fine and well mannered and cultured. And you..." He gestured up and down the length of her. "You're a Lady now. I have no right to expect you to be the same person you were three years ago. You owe me nothing. You're to be wed to another and it's improper for you to be in my room. You should leave."

She didn't want this. She couldn't just walk away now. Her gaze drifted around the room as she grasped for something to say. She turned her eyes to the floor in an effort to hold back her tears. Blinking several times, she reached down and lifted the aged parchment that he'd dropped.

"Don't!" He took a step forward.

She flipped over the portrait. It was her. She was younger, but it was her. She stared at the expert lines, the curve of her mouth, the crinkles in the corner of her eyes. It had been drawn by an expert hand.

"When did you do this?"

He swallowed hard and covered his eyes.

She took a step closer. "Jamen, when did you draw this?"

"The week after I… last spoke to you."

She stared at the portrait in disbelief. "You did this from memory?"

He shrugged.

"It's beautiful." It was like seeing herself through his eyes. He'd shown her pictures he'd done before, but they'd been of landscapes and animals, never of people.

"You want it, keep it," he said. "I have dozens more at the Manor House, I can send them to you as a wedding present and you can give them to Edward."

His words pierced her to the core. "Jamen!"

Before she could finish he crossed to her in one stride and fisted his hand in her hair. He crushed his lips down on hers and yanked her body against his. Her mind whirled as she took in his scent of alcohol and leather. His familiar frame pressed against hers made her tingle. He pried her lips apart with his tongue and her knees buckled. She clung to him in an effort to keep from falling. Need shot straight to her core, making her body hum. His arousal pressed against her belly and her skin heated. Their tongues mingled and entwined the way they used to. Familiar. Passionate. Meant to be together. Then suddenly, he was gone.

She opened her eyes, swayed and clutched the corner of a chair for support.

He shook his head, his face full of regret. "I'm sorry, Scarlet, I shouldn't have—"

"No, it's fine." Her mind still swam in the aftermath. The room spun and her body pulsed with need. The fire of his kiss made all reason and learning fly out the window. She wanted more.

"I'm sorry, Lettie. Sorry that you had to see me like this. Sorry that I hurt you, that this is who I turned out to be. That I couldn't be what you needed me to be. Sorry I can't give you—" He gestured around the room. "All of this."

She shook her head trying to catch her bearings. "Jamen—"

A tear leaked from his eye and then he tore into the adjoining bathing room and slammed the door.

She stared after him, assaulted by memories of their one night together. His strong hands on her hips, guiding her, showing her the way as she straddled him. His moist hot breath on her neck as he kissed his way down her body. The smell of her sheets and the musky scent of his skin.

The moan that escaped her, snapped her to the present. She couldn't do this. She owed her aunt. They'd worked too hard.

She smoothed her hands over her dress trying to rid herself of the slick moisture on them. She picked the dropped portrait off the floor and stared at it again. After several seconds she set the drawing in his satchel and turned for the door. Tears rolled down her cheeks. She finally understood. For as much as he had ruined her, she had been his ruin as well.

CHAPTER EIGHT

Edward and his companions departed the next morning. Still plagued by seeing Jamen so drunk, Scarlet thought it best if she didn't see him so soon, so she'd sent word to Edward that she was resting from a headache. He'd come to her immediately and wished her a speedy recovery. Then he'd kissed her. Really kissed her, for the first time. But the kiss only left her numb. Despite her aunt's warnings, she wanted to love Edward. To find joy in his companionship and desire at his touch, but she didn't.

As soon as she heard the hoofbeats ride away, she went down to eat. It had been days since she'd had a real meal and her stomach growled like a bear.

In the kitchen, she talked with the servants trying to pry information from them about Edward. They seemed reluctant to say a cross word about the man whose father paid their wages.

While she ate, Camille prepared Aunt Liza a pot of tea and then they walked upstairs together.

Aunt Liza's condition had worsened further. Scarlet mopped her aunt's brow with a cool rag. Liza's complexion had ashened and her breathing was shallow.

"More tea?" Camille asked.

"No. No more tea," Scarlet replied. "She's not keeping it down. Where's the doctor?"

"I don't know," said the maid. "Master Lyden said he would send someone, but that was this morning."

"Well, we'll have to send someone again then."

"The men have all gone hunting, M'lady."

Fear crawled up Scarlet's nape making her hair stand on end. She couldn't lose Aunt Liza. "What about the head house servant? Where is he?"

"He…he went with them, Lady Scarlet."

"It's all right, my dear. I'll be fine." Aunt Liza's voice was barely a whisper. "Don't worry yourself about me. You should be celebrating and getting ready for your wedding."

"No." Scarlet shook her head. "I won't celebrate until you are better."

"Don't be foolish, girl," said Liza. "You've come too far to ruin it now."

"Who's in charge?" Scarlet asked Camille.

The maid looked from Scarlet to Aunt Liza and back. "You're in charge I believe, M'lady."

Dammit! Her aunt needed a doctor. Her mind whirled as she tried to figure out what to do.

"I'll go myself," she said finally. "You stay here and see to Aunt

Liza."

Scarlet stood and shoved the small towel into Camille's hand. Marching to the armoire she pulled out her riding cloak and fastened it in place. "Keep her cool and comfortable. I'll return soon as soon as I'm able."

"Yes, M'lady."

"Scarlet no, you can't go. It's too dangerous for you to ride alone." Her aunt's eyes widened in fear. "Wait for Edward."

"I'll be fine." She smiled. "I grew up here, remember? I've ridden through all of Westfall more times than I can count."

Her aunt opened her mouth to say something and broke into a fit of coughing. The maid rushed to her side and gave Liza a sip of tea.

"I'll be back as soon as I can," said Scarlet.

She looked at her aunt once more, before stepping out into the hallway. If she lost Aunt Liza... She couldn't lose Aunt Liza. She needed her. Aunt Liza knew the truth about what had happened to Scarlet. The only one she could talk to on her bad days. The strength at Scarlet's back. The only mother figure Scarlet had known in the past three years.

Scarlet rushed down the stairs to the front hall. A young servant boy stood near the door.

"Is there a stable hand to ready a horse?"

"Yes, M'lady, but the horses are all gone," said the boy. "Sir Malcolm and Master Edward took them all for the hunt."

Scarlet's heart pounded in her chest. How could this be

happening? "I have my Aunt Liza's horse." Her voice cracked with emotion.

"I'm sorry, but Master Lyden took her as well. Said he needed a horse to carry the supplies."

Scarlet stamped her foot and pulled on her hair by the roots. How could he dare to take her aunt's horse? This couldn't be happening.

"Lord Gwyn's steed is the only one here I'm afraid."

Scarlet's hand shot out and grabbed the boy. "Lord Gwyn? Did he not go with Edward?"

"No, M'lady. He stayed behind."

"Where is he?"

The boy's eyes widened in fear. "In his room I believe—"

Scarlet tore up the stairs and down the hall. She banged on the door and waited. She banged again and the door opened.

He wore the same tunic and breeches from the previous night. His dark curly hair was its normal mess and his eyes were unusually sunken in. The stubble upon his chin had grown thicker. He blinked at her several times and then glanced down the hall.

"Lady Scarlet—"

"Lord Gwyn, I need Brutin. My aunt is sick and I need to fetch the doctor."

"Surely there is a servant—"

Her patience wore thin. "Jamen!" She stepped into his space. After what had transpired between them the previous night she had no right to ask for his help. A tear stung her cheek. "Please, Jamen. I

86

think she's dying."

His eyes cleared in an instant. "Let me get my cloak."

"Thank you," she managed between sobs. She swiped at her cheeks and took several deep breaths.

He returned a moment later, cloak already on, a satchel slung over his shoulder, sword in hand.

"Has she gotten no better?" he asked as they hurried down the stairs.

"No. Her skin is colorless and her breathing is so light that it's hard to tell if she's breathing at all."

They reached the front hall and Jamen rounded the staircase and headed toward the back of the house. She had to run to keep up with him. They strode through the kitchen to an exterior door. Jamen threw his cloak over his shoulders as they exited and made for the stable. Despite her anxiety, a thrill traversed her body at the sight of his forceful, take-charge attitude. It was completely opposite of Edward.

"Does she have any kind of odor?" Jamen asked.

"Odor?" She couldn't concentrate.

"Yes. Does she smell sweet, or sour or something else?"

"Sweet, I think." She walked as fast as she could to keep up. The snow on the hard packed ground made her shoes slip. She let out a yelp and Jamen caught her by the elbow before she went down.

"Sweet like what?" he asked, pulling her upright again.

"I don't know." His touch heated her skin. "Why?"

"Because it sounds like poison."

Scarlet's stomach soured. "Poison?"

"Come on." He took her hand. She allowed him to lead her toward the stable.

Jamen retrieved Brutin and saddled him. Who would want to poison her aunt? Jamen had to be wrong. It couldn't be poison.

He led his horse outside and mounted it. He held his hand out to her. "Come on."

Scarlet stepped up to the animal. It whinnied and pawed at the ground. Jamen reined him in and held his hand out to Scarlet once more. She placed her hand in his firm grip and he swung her up behind him. Instinctively she wrapped her arms around his waist, her body pressing into his wool cloak. Her thighs wrapped around his and her core pressed into his backside. A jolt of energy shot through her at his nearness. Gods have mercy, but she almost wanted him to tackle her to the ground and take her right there.

No, Stop! She couldn't think like that. She'd made a promise to Aunt Liza and to Edward. She had a duty to them and one must always do her duty.

Jamen spurred Brutin forward and they shot off around the corner of the house. Scarlet grabbed on tighter, laying her head on Jamen's back. She squeezed him with her whole body. Once more, memories of their one night together burst from the cage she'd kept them in.

The soft way he'd kissed her flesh. The feel of his skin on hers as they'd become one. His intense eyes that stared into hers as they both reached climax. Scarlet shook her head. Never before, and never since, had she felt so connected to another person. She doubted that she'd ever feel so connected to Edward.

It didn't matter though, she reminded herself. She was marrying Edward for comfort and security, not for pleasure.

"I'm sorry about last night," she said softly.

"What?" he asked, spurring the horse onward.

"I said, I'm sorry about last night." She bit her lip and waited for a response.

"It's my fault. I shouldn't have been drinking. You have nothing to apologize for."

*****

Jamen tried to concentrate on where he was going, but it was difficult with Scarlet's arms around him. The warmth of her soft body pressed into him, sparking his arousal.

Now was no time to be thinking of intimacies, but he couldn't help it. It felt so familiar having her near. Her scent wafted over his shoulder and filled him. Rosewater as always. His heart ached even more for dreams that could not be.

The night before, what he could remember of it, had been a disaster. He'd never wanted her to see him like that and the things he'd said to her... There was no making it any better. After locking himself in the bathing room in an effort to keep from seeing the pain he caused her, yet again, he'd finally been faced to force the truth. Edward was the best choice for her.

He understood finally why she'd chosen Edward. Because

Edward would never hurt her.

But there was no time to think about that now. He needed to get his wits about him. Especially since if he was correct, not only was her aunt in danger, Scarlet was as well.

Her aunt hadn't gotten sick until arriving at Sir Malcolm's estate, which meant that someone meant her harm and in return meant Scarlet harm. And he wasn't going to allow someone to hurt her. He'd do whatever he had to, to make sure of that. Including going against Scarlet herself.

An hour later Jamen pulled his horse up to the doctor's hut and slid off. He tied Brutin to a post and reached for Scarlet. She set her hands on his shoulder and he grabbed her small waist and helped her to the ground. She looked at him and his chest tightened.

"Thank you," she said.

"Come on." He took her hand and together they rushed to the doctor's front door. Jamen stepped up on the porch and knocked. Scarlet wrapped her arms around herself and waited.

"She'll be all right," Jamen said.

"I don't think so," she replied.

He knocked on the door again and it swung open slightly. The smell of blood tickled his nostrils. Jamen tensed. There were no lights on inside.

"Hello?" he called.

No answer.

He pounded to his horse and pulled his sword from his pack.

"What is it?" She ran to meet him. "What's wrong?"

"Stay here." He stared at her until she nodded, hugging herself tighter.

Jamen took several cautious steps toward the hut. The door creaked as he pushed it wider with the tip of his sword.

"Doctor?" he called. "Doctor, are you home?"

He advanced into the hut. The stench of blood invaded him. He scanned the room and located a lantern on the mantle. He crossed to it, his boots sticking to the wooden planks. When he struck a match and the room illuminated, a high-pitched scream sounded to his left. He turned to find Scarlet clutching her mouth in terror.

Gazing around he took in the horrific scene. In the middle of the room, both the doctor and his wife lay in pools of drying blood. It had seeped into the floorboards, causing his boots to stick. Next to the doctor scrawled in the blood was the word, "Vampire."

"Get back." He waved to Scarlet.

She didn't move, transfixed.

He strode to her grabbed her by the arm, guiding her outside. She crumpled on the porch with a thump. He stood motionless for a minute, before moving to her side and crouching in front of her.

Scarlet's face crumbled and she began to sob.

Dammit! This was just the kind of horror he'd tried to keep from her. "Don't...don't cry. Everything is going to be fine." He reached out and put a hand on her shoulder. His mind calculated what he'd seen, trying to figure out his next move.

Every fiber of his being wanted to hug her. To hold her close and comfort her.

"Lettie, stop crying."

She didn't.

"Scarlet," he said again. He shifted on the balls of his feet and rubbed the back of his neck. He hadn't had much experience calming a sobbing woman. "Scarlet, stop," he ordered.

He wiped the tears from her eyes. "I need you to stay put this time."

She nodded and pulled her legs in tight.

Jamen stood and blew out a huge breath. His legs tingled as the blood rushed into them. He clutched his sword and entered the hut once more.

Everything seemed to be in its place. In the corner, a cabinet full of medicinal supplies was open, but there were no signs of a struggle.

Jamen sniffed the air and listened for sounds of the intruder. He checked the kitchen area as well as the bedroom, but the assailant was gone. Setting his sword on the table he walked to the bodies, crouched down and closed the doctor's eyes. Jamen turned the doctor's head and a large precise wound marred his throat. The wife sported the same injuries.

The hair on Jamen's arms prickled as he looked at the word written in the blood. He glanced at the doctor's fingers and frowned. There was no blood on them. The wife's fingers were clean as well.

He strode from the hut. Scarlet continued to hug herself but she tracked him to where he stopped by Brutin.

"Are they dead?" she asked.

"Yes."

"Did…did…vampires kill them?"

The terror she exuded tugged at his heart. This was why he was a Vampire Slayer. To keep her and Westfall safe. Problem was, vampires didn't do this.

"Don't worry. I'm going to fix this."

"How?" she asked.

"Trust me." He searched in his saddlebag.

Scarlet got to her feet and stepped to the edge of the porch. "Are you a doctor? Do you know where one is? This doctor is dead by vampires that aren't suppose to exist and we have no one else to help my aunt."

He stopped faced her. He bit the inside of his cheek. "I'm not a healer but I know where another one is."

"Where?"

Jamen rubbed his fingers through his hair and then looked up at the sky. Clouds hovered above like giant centennials. He needed to let Tanah Darah know what was happening. The implications of calling this a vampire attack could be devastating. It didn't make any sense. Why would someone want to blame vampires?

He looked at Scarlet. This couldn't wait, he needed to talk to Snow now but he was positive that if he asked Scarlet to stay put, she wouldn't obey. Doing this would bring her into his world whether he liked it or not.

"Gerall has healing skills," he said.

Suspicion crept over her features. "You said Gerall wasn't in Westfall."

"He isn't, but I can get word to him—"

"How? That could take weeks, Aunt Liza doesn't have weeks."

Jamen looked around. There wasn't anyone in the area. He had no choice, he had to do this now. From inside his pack he pulled out a garnet ring and a hand mirror with an identical stone. He sighed and then walked to where Scarlet waited.

"What is that?"

"It's a mirror and a ring." He slipped on the red stone ring.

She stared at it. "Where did you get it?"

"From my brother-in-law, Sage."

Her eyebrows knit together. "Your brother-in-law? Snow married?"

Jamen shifted uncomfortably. "Yes."

Snow had explained to him how to work the mirror to contact them; he'd never actually done it himself though.

He pressed the red stone on the top of the hand mirror and then touched the ring to it. The surface shimmered and his stomach turned, remembering the last time he'd had to use mirror travel. He had been through a mirror once. A sensation he was not ready to repeat.

"Snow Gwyn of Tanah Darah," he commanded. The surface shimmered and then dozens of mirrors appeared. The image flew by mirror after mirror until it finally landed on a large ornate one.

Because he and his brothers had to travel between Tanah Darah and Gwyn Manor, Sage and Snow had moved the garden mirror into the castle where it could be monitored for activity.

"By the gods..." Scarlet stared into the mirror. "How did you–"

The image rotated until Jamen stared into the great hall of Tanah Darah. A sentry stood on either side.

"Queen Snow," he yelled.

The sentries turned. Beside him Scarlet gasped, but he said nothing.

"It's Jamen, I need my sister, and Sage."

One of the vampire sentries nodded and ran out of the hall.

"Is that— Are they—" Scarlet's wide eyes stared into the mirror.

"They're vampires," said Jamen.

"And your sister?"

Jamen sighed. "She is Queen of Tanah Darah. Her husband's name is Sage."

Scarlet's brow furrowed. "But you said—"

"Jamen!"

His gaze turned back to the mirror.

"Is something wrong?" Snow asked.

"What's happened?" Sage stepped beside her.

"We have a problem in Westfall. There's been a murder and the word 'vampire' was written in the blood."

Sage and Snow exchanged a look.

"It's not possible," said Sage.

"It wasn't vampires who did this. There's blood all over the room and vampires don't waste like that. The wounds are too clean and neither of the victims have blood on their fingers from having written the word, so it could've only been done by the person who killed them. Besides, it was most likely someone they knew, there are no signs of a struggle."

"So someone is trying to accuse us?" asked Snow.

"Looks like. Have you had any problems since I left?"

"A group is making the trek back with Erik but we haven't heard anything," said Sage.

"I need your help. I need a healer."

"What's happened?" Panic etched Snow's features.

"I'm fine. The victims were the doctor and his wife and Scarlet's aunt is sick. I think she may have been poisoned."

"Scarlet? I don't understand—"

"Snow, I don't have much time. I need Gerall to come to Westfall. I can meet him at the lake and break a hole through the ice so he can come through."

Snow shook her head. "It's too risky. You'd have to make sure the ice was broken all the way to the mirror at the bottom without breaking the mirror itself or he could get stuck inside. That's why Erik went down to help our people get back safely."

Jamen cursed a blue streak. "Well, I hope they return before someone discovers these bodies," said Jamen. "Is there any way to get a hold of King Adrian? His healer woman, can she come?"

"It would take too much time," Snow said. "We wouldn't be able to get to them before nightfall. It would be faster for you to go yourself."

"I don't know that I'll be welcomed."

"Of course you will. You're my brother. King Adrian and Queen Redlynn will be sure to help," replied Sage.

Jamen's gut clenched. Sage thought of him as a brother. It was comforting yet strange.

A ride to Wolvenglen Forest would take several hours at least. And the wolves were fiercely protective of their mates. It was unlikely at best that their healer would be allowed to leave with him.

He was running out of options.

"What if I took the mirror and let Gerall look over Scarlet's aunt. Then he could tell me what I needed to do."

"I don't think so. If you really want to help her, the best thing to do is to go to Wolvenglen."

"I understand. Thank you." He went to turn off the mirror.

"Jamen?"

He stopped.

"I'm sorry." Snow's gaze held a volume of words that she didn't say.

He nodded and then pushed the red stone on the mirror and it went dark. He stared at it a moment longer. Going to Wolvenglen was not something he wanted to do.

"It's true," Scarlet said.

"Yes." He walked to Brutin and put the mirror and ring into the saddlebag.

Scarlet grabbed his arm. "Jamen—"

"I have to go to Wolvenglen Forest. I need to speak to King

Adrian to see if he will allow his healer Hanna to come to your aunt."

"I'm coming with you."

"No." Jamen shook his head. "It's too dangerous. I'll take you back to the estate."

Scarlet stepped between him and Brutin and planted her hands on her hips. Her expression made Jamen smile inwardly. The spark in her eyes was the old Scarlet.

"Now you listen to me, Jamen Gwyn. Taking me back to the estate and then going on to Wolvenglen Forest will take more time. Precious time that could be better spent with your healer."

As if she'd wished for it, snow began to fall and hit him lightly on the shoulders.

"Dammit, Scarlet, this is why I broke it off to begin with. I didn't want you involved."

"Well I'm involved now whether we like it or not, so get used to it. Where you go, I go."

"Really?" He stepped in so close that the warmth of her body met his. "Just moments ago I had to almost slap you to get you to stop crying when you saw two dead bodies. What you are going to do when you see something worse?"

She stood taller and lifted her chin. "I'll be fine. This was a shock, that's all. I can handle myself."

"Oh really? My sister thought she could handle herself as well and look where she ended up for her stupidity."

Scarlet narrowed her eyes and her jaw tightened. "Did you just

98

say I'm stupid?"

Jamen blinked rapidly. "What? No I—"

"Yes, you did. You said that I was stupid for thinking I could take care of myself. I'll have you know that the only reason I'm in the position I am with a nobleman for a fiancé was because of me. I did that."

"Coming into my world isn't like flirting your way into the arms of a rich husband Scarlet."

Her jaw dropped and her eyes widened. "No, but if it's anything like handling you, I think I can hold my own."

Jamen's mouth opened and closed. Speechless again.

Gods above. He didn't want her anywhere near this. Not the wolves, not the vampires, not even him.

She cocked her head to the side and pursed her lips. Jamen turned from her and stomped the ground into submission. He cursed and yelled and cursed some more. How did she do this to him? He should just tie her to the post and wait for someone to find her for all the trouble she was.

He hung his head, defeated. He couldn't leave her. They didn't know who had killed the doctor or why. If it had anything to do with the sudden illness of her aunt, she would be in danger as well. And with snow falling...

"Fine."

He mounted his horse and waited. Anger heated his body until it stifled him. He tried to slow the thundering of his heart.

Scarlet coughed but he continued to stare straight ahead.

"Really, Jamen, you are being such a baby about this. And the time that we waste arguing about this, my aunt could be dying."

He looked at her and growled. Reaching down her pulled her up.

She settled behind him. Again a feeling of comfort seeped over him as she slid her arms around him and laid her cheek on his back. He closed his eyes. The gods must really hate him.

CHAPTER NINE

As they rode into the courtyard of Wolvenglen castle it finally hit Scarlet. Everything he'd told her was true.

On their long ride through Westfall and then north through Wolvenglen Forest, she'd convinced herself that it couldn't be possible. There was no way that everything he'd said about Fae magick and Vampire Slayers could be true. But here she was. At a castle that shouldn't exist. About to go meet a Werewolf King, who should only be a fairytale.

Jamen dismounted and helped her down and a jolt shot through her as her feet hit the ground. Her legs and back were stiff with cold from having sat for so long. The snow fell heavily and blanketed everything. Her cloak had soaked through and she shivered in the chilly, damp air.

Jamen handed his horse to a large burly man and nodded. The man exuded a power that she had never felt before. His gaze tracked her every movement. He lifted his nose in the air and sniffed. Jamen took her arm in his.

"Stay close," he whispered.

A wave of apprehension rushed through her and she clutched his hand.

They were half way up the steps when the doors opened and a tall well-built man with dark wavy hair stepped out. Next to him, a flame-haired beauty with golden eyes.

"Jamen Gwyn," the man said.

"King Adrian. Queen Redlynn." Jamen bowed, pulling Scarlet down with him. She stumbled and hit the coarse stone steps with a yelp. She yanked her hand from Jamen's and shot him an icy look.

"What brings you into the woods? Is there a problem in Tanah Darah?" asked Adrian.

"No, King," Jamen said.

Adrian waved them up. "Come on now, I've never had people bow to me before outside my pack. It makes me nervous. Besides, it's just Adrian. Get up and tell us what you need."

Scarlet stood and smoothed her dress. The front was caked in mud and snow. Aunt Liza would be most displeased. She wondered of the state of her hair and face. Oh, what did it matter? For once she had more important problems than her looks.

"I have need of a healer," said Jamen. "The one in Westfall is dead."

"A healer? Of course," said Redlynn. "Please, come in, the air is damp and you must be chilled to your marrow."

"Did you say dead?" asked Adrian.

"I did. And thank you, Queen, but I'm afraid this is urgent

business and we must leave as quickly as we came. You see, this is Lady Scarlet. Her aunt has taken ill. I believe she's been poisoned and I wondered if Hanna might accompany us back to tend to her."

Adrian and Redlynn exchanged a look and then Redlynn's gaze swept to Scarlet. "Come warm yourselves inside while we discuss it."

"Please." Scarlet stepped forward. "My aunt is very dear to me. I don't have much money, but I can pay—"

"Payment is not the issue," said Adrian. "We'll discuss it inside."

Several men had gathered at the entrance and stared at her. Scarlet took a step closer to Jamen. Her apprehension was overwhelming. Where were the women? Why had only men come out? Jamen placed his arm around her shoulder. The feel of it comforted her slightly.

There seemed to be no choice. If they wanted the wolves' help, they had to go in.

"Come on." Jamen looked at Scarlet. "You haven't eaten in hours. Let's at least eat before we leave. I know you're stiff from the ride."

Scarlet held her breath. The prospect of being in a werewolf castle shook her to the core.

He gave her a half-hearted smile then lifted her hand and kissed it. "Trust me."

Scarlet sat at a long wooden table next to a large roaring fire butterflies fluttering in her belly. Her knee bounced under the table. She needed to get back to her aunt.

An enormous tree decorated in beautiful wooden sculptures of animals and houses stood in the corner. Underneath a pile of presents spilled across the floor. Everything smelled of pine and sweet spices. She smiled to herself remembering the gingerbread she used to help her mother make each year.

Above the fireplace hung a beautifully ornate mirror. Bows of holly and ivy adorned it in celebration of Yuletide Festivus. In all the commotion of the wedding and her aunt's illness, she'd almost forgotten about the holiday.

All around the hall hung antlers in every shape and size. Now she knew where to send the antlers from her wedding feast buck, as a thank you.

A shiver ran through her and her thoughts turned to Edward. How in the world would she explain all of this to him? It surprised her how she hadn't had a single thought of him since leaving Westfall. But that's how it was with Edward.

Jamen was all consuming, passion and fire and grit. He stuck in her bones and threaded into her muscles as if he'd always been a part of her. Edward just...was. She barely spared him a thought when she wasn't in his presence or actively trying to figure out how to best keep him complacent. Even so, she'd made a promise to marry him. If she broke it, what would happen to her aunt? What would happen to her? She couldn't even consider it.

"Here you are." A young woman of about eighteen brought a

plate of food and set it in front of her.

"Thank you," said Jamen. He grabbed his plate and pulled it close, picked up a chicken leg and bit into it.

Scarlet's stomach growled and she followed suit. She downed her chicken with a glass of warm mead. The honeyed wine sparkled on her tongue and slid down her throat. It was delicious.

After several minutes King Adrian and Queen Redlynn entered the hall, and sat across from them.

"I'm sorry," said Adrian, his expression dark. "Hanna cannot go."

Scarlet's heart sank. "But my aunt—"

He held up a hand. "I understand. I do. But you must understand as well. Wolves and their mates share a special bond. When a mate is away it is hard on both parties. Hanna's mate is a special case. He does especially bad when she's away. Even if it was only for the day, I am afraid that I couldn't guarantee that he wouldn't show up to get her. Besides the fact that they have several young and he doesn't do well with them on his own. Even with all of us helping out, there is no guarantee of what he might do."

Scarlet pushed her plate away. "So there's nothing you can do?"

"I didn't say that," said Adrian. He glanced at Redlynn.

"My mother was a healer and I have extensive knowledge of herbs and tinctures and such. I can't guarantee that I can cure her, but I will go with you."

"We'll take it, with great thanks, Queen Redlynn." Jamen inclined his head.

"Redlynn," she replied. "I'm just Redlynn."

"We should go as soon as possible," Scarlet said.

"And you will," said Adrian. "But not tonight."

Scarlet stood. "But we must—"

"I'm afraid it's impossible. The snow is coming down quite hard. If you leave now, you'll get stuck in the storm. Better to wait till morning."

Time was wasting away for her aunt as they just sat and ate. "My aunt could be dead by then."

Adrian nodded. "Unfortunately, that is true. But getting the three of you stuck out in a snowstorm, without shelter, could kill all of you as well. You may be willing to take that chance in which case I wish you the best, but I will not risk Redlynn." He reached over and clasped Redlynn's hand.

Scarlet opened her mouth to argue, but Jamen laid his hand on her arm.

"Thank you. We appreciate your hospitality as well as your help. We'll wait till first light and see how the weather fairs."

Scarlet glared at him. If it was his family in danger, would he say the same? How could he just sit there and do nothing? "Jamen—"

He turned to her. "We will wait." His eyes hardened and her cheeks heated.

She had several choice words she was dying to say. She bit her cheek in an effort to hold them at bay.

Redlynn stood and smiled at Scarlet. "Why don't you come with me. I can show you to your room. We'll bring up water so you can bathe and you can borrow one of my dresses till yours dries."

She looked down at her plate of half eaten food, but her stomach felt like she'd eaten a rock.

"Go. I'll check on you in a while," Jamen said.

She nodded and followed Redlynn.

*****

Jamen kept his gaze trained on Scarlet as she followed Redlynn out of sight. Her worry for her aunt was more than apparent and he hoped that tomorrow wouldn't be too late.

Unfortunately, that wasn't the worst of his problems.

Staying the night with the wolves could cause people to talk. He didn't care what anyone in Sir Malcolm's household said about him. As for Scarlet… that was another thing all together. For the first time in a long time he was glad that he was a Lord of Westfall. It may be that very thing that would save her reputation at this point.

"You love her." Adrian poured himself a cup of mead.

"I did once." Jamen picked the piece of bread from his plate and bit into it.

"You lie to yourself if you think you do not still love her." Adrian watched Jamen for a moment and then held up his hands. "Any wolf here can smell your affection a mile away. She feels the same you know." He crossed his arms over his chest.

Jamen shook his head. "Not anymore. I broke her. Killed her spirit. Shamed her in the worst way."

"You'd be surprised how much a woman can bear. I do not

doubt your words, but I looked into her eyes. That is not a broken woman."

Adrian's words may be true, but it didn't matter. Jamen couldn't afford to put her in danger and she was engaged to Edward. Assuming that Edward and his family had nothing to do with the poisoning of Lady Eliza, he would leave her to her vows. And go back to what he did best. Killing vampires.

"How is your sister adjusting?" Adrian picked a grape off of Scarlet's plate and popped it into his mouth.

"Well, surprisingly. It is the rest of us that are having a hard time moving on. Have you heard anything from Dax?" Jamen held his breath.

Adrian shook his head. "Not in some time. Don't worry about your brother Flint. Dax will keep him safe. If there was trouble, Dax would send word."

Jamen nodded. He didn't know the werebear Dax all that well, but from what he'd seen, Dax was an honorable man and could hold his own in a fight. Together he and Flint would make a formidable team.

"You don't mind Redlynn coming with us?" Jamen asked.

Adrian shrugged. "I don't have much of a choice. Redlynn is my mate, my love, my life. But I've learned that when she makes her mind up about something, I cannot stop her. She has a caring heart and doesn't like to see people in pain. Though she never wanted to be a healer, she's becoming quite a good one. Besides, Sage is my friend and you are his family. Our lands have only just begun to see peace after centuries of war. It wouldn't bode well for our alliance were I not to offer help."

Jamen inclined his head. "I am in your debt."

"No," Adrian laughed. "You are in my mate's."

Jamen raised his mug of mead and then gulped it down.

An hour later Redlynn showed Jamen to his room.

"Lady Scarlet is right next door." She pointed.

"I'd like to thank you for your generous offer to come with us. I hope it won't be too much of an inconvenience to you and your family."

Redlynn smiled. "I recently weaned our youngest. It will be nice to get away before Adrian decides it's time to try for another. And I'm sure with me being gone for a few days he will want to start as soon as I return." She laughed.

"How many do you have?"

"We have four now. Three girls and a boy. But Adrian won't be happy till we have a dozen or more."

Jamen chuckled.

Her golden eyes studied him. "Do you want children Jamen?"

Regret darkened his thoughts. "I would love children, but it seems life has other plans for me."

She smiled slightly and her gaze traveled to Scarlet's door. "I wouldn't say that."

He followed Redlynn's gaze. "Well, I thank you anyway for your help."

"Goodnight, Jamen," she said.

"Goodnight, Redlynn."

She turned down the hall.

When she'd disappeared, he opened his door. To his relief, the room was nothing like what he was forced to endure at Sir Malcolm's. It felt more like home. There was a simple bed with a plush blanket. Clean towels hung near a washbasin. A bathing tub filled with water sat in a corner, steaming. He sniffed himself. He smelled of horse and sweat. Stripping off his tunic and breeches he walked to the tub. Maybe a hot bath would help him keep his mind off of his current situation.

Jamen slid down and let the water flow over him. The heat of it relaxed his muscles and cleared his mind. He plunged his face under and wet his hair. A crude bar of soap sat on a chair next to the tub. He reached out and grabbed it. The oily bar smelled of lemon and mint. He rubbed it under his armpits and between his legs. The refreshing bar cooled his skin.

He lathered his body, relaxing further. Sitting back he let his mind wander. It was strange that Scarlet's aunt fell sick, possibly poisoned, and the one man able to help her was dead. There was no doubt in his mind that the two were connected, but why blame vampires? He didn't know how all the pieces fit together. That was Gerall's department.

A soft knock on the door had him out of the tub in an instant.

"Jamen?"

"Uh…just a moment." He slipped across the floor, barely

making it to the towels by the basin as the door opened. He whipped the fabric around his lower half. Scarlet looked around the room for him.

Upon spotting him her face flushed peachy. "Oh! I'm so sorry. I didn't realize…" She turned her face away. "I'll come back later."

"No. It's fine. Come in."

"I really shouldn't—"

"Scarlet, it's fine. Just let me get on my breeches." He located his breeches where he'd dropped them. She closed the door, and pressed her forehead into it until he finished getting them on. "You can turn around now." He dried his hair with the towel.

She peeked at him and then turned. Her loose, damp hair hung naturally to her shoulders. The simple cotton dress she wore dragged on the floor due to her petite frame. Beneath it, the silhouette of her body called to him. He could just see the round curve of her breasts and the small buds that formed from rubbing against the fabric.

He cleared his throat and clutched the towel in front of his waist so she wouldn't see his growing arousal. Why did she have to be so damned beautiful?

"I just came to thank you." She fingered the sides of the dress. "For helping my aunt. I know I haven't been the most cooperative. And I was most unkind downstairs, but I'm just so worried about her. I can't imagine losing her. She means more to me than— Anyway, I appreciate what you are doing for us. For me."

"Of course." He set the towel on the chair. "I'd do anything to help and I won't stop until I find out who hurt her and killed the doctor."

She met his gaze and then took several slow steps toward him. A tingling sensation settled in his groin and the hairs on the nape of his neck stood on end. Tentatively she reached out and ran her hand over a large scar across his chest.

"It's true isn't it? The vampires, the werewolves, the fae woman. All of it." Her eyes met his and she was the young eager girl he'd known, once more.

"Yes." His voice came out horse and strained.

She swirled her fingertips over the scar on his collarbone and then up the one on his neck. The sensation sent shockwaves of pleasure rippling through him. Her caress was light as a feather but touched him deep in his bones.

"How? How could we not have known?"

"Because we were blind. And because they didn't want to be known."

Her warm palm settled on his chest. "Tell me again why you left me."

He swallowed hard and caught her by the wrist. Her lips parted and she let out a breathy moan that had him almost take her right there.

"What does it matter? You are to be married to another."

Her eyes pleaded with him. "Tell me," she whispered.

He'd never been able to deny her before. She was so close and this was his chance. His chance to set things right with her and make her understand. To be forgiven, so they could both move on.

"That night," he began. "After we'd… made love I went home." He rubbed a circle on the underside of her wrist. The skin was so delicate and soft. He stared at her lips and she licked them.

"My brothers and Snow had gathered in the solar, waiting for me. A cloaked woman sat waiting as well. She told us of the calling. The calling of a Slayer. It was only ever bestowed on a family of nobility and honor, where there were at least five children born. She said that the nine ancient prophecies would soon begin to be fulfilled. That evil that sat on the throne of Tanah Darah and it must be destroyed or all of Fairelle would be lost. Then one by one she placed her hands on us and uttered words I still cannot understand. I spent the entire night and the following day, agonizing over what had happened and what it would mean. For me…for you. I thought that by giving you up I was keeping you safe. Giving you a better life than the one I could provide."

He lifted her wrist to his nose and inhaled her sweet skin. Every cell in his body screamed out for her, while every rational thought told him to stop.

"I remember the first time you held my hand," she said. "I was sixteen and you were nineteen. We were in the apple orchard and you had invited me on a picnic."

He rubbed his cheek against her wrist. "You wore a dress the color of a robin's egg and had pinned your hair up, exposing your neck." He reached out and ran his hand over her slender throat. He squeezed it lightly, feeling her pulse in his grasp.

He took in every inch of her face. From the soft line of her nose, to the curve of her lips. It was unreal to think that she was here, and he was here. Desire shook him down to the soles of his feet.

"Scarlet—"

"Don't." She pressed her palm onto his lips. "Don't say anything." Her eyes glowed with need. She traced his lips with her fingers and he pulled her close, wrapping his arm around her back like he had when they'd danced. She sucked in a breath as he pressed his body against hers.

Doing this would bring shame upon her and upon his family's honor if they were caught, but at that moment, nothing else mattered but her.

"For so long I waited for you to return to me," she said. "I dreamed that you would tell me you made a mistake. Even though I hated you for what you'd done. I wanted you back." Sadness shadowed her features.

He had made a mistake, but it didn't matter. They couldn't go back and she couldn't be his now. "I wish I could take it back, but it was for the best. Even now it is dangerous for you to be with me. You see the world I live in. The people I must deal with. You would never be safe."

"Safe? Am I truly safe if someone in Edward's house poisoned my aunt?"

He already knew the answer.

"I came to find you once," she said. "I'd heard you were in the tavern so I came to speak to you."

His heartbeat quickened. "I never saw you."

"No, you didn't. You were hips deep inside some harlot over a barrel in back of the tavern."

A cry of anguish escaped him. Humiliation chilled him to the bone. She'd seen him. At his worst, his lowest point, she been there and witnessed it.

"That was the night I fled to my Aunt Liza's."

"Lettie, I—"

She yanked on his neck and pressed his lips into hers. She plunged her tongue deep in his mouth and a guttural sound rumbled in his chest.

Pressing his palm into the small of her back he brought her closer still. Her soft body clung to his, her petite frame nestling his arousal in the softness of her belly.

She broke her lips free of him. He pinned her neck in place with his hand and kissed down the side of her throat while skimming his palm over the curve of her breast.

He didn't care anymore. It didn't matter that they shouldn't. All that mattered was that she was his again.

*****

Scarlet's mind whirled in a dizzying fog of pleasure so strong that she couldn't think straight. To have him in her arms again. To feel his lips on her skin. It was all like the fantasy she'd imagined, over and over and over.

He lifted her from the ground and carried her to the bed, his body covering hers. His taut muscles that had once been lean and long were now hard beneath her fingertips. His whiskers scratched

115

her face and left her lips raw as he pressed his mouth against hers. Her body flushed with heat at his nearness. His musky scent floated around her while the sweet taste of mead tantalized her mouth. So long she'd wanted to be with him again. Jamen, her Jamen.

She kneaded the muscles of his back. He lifted the hem of her dress and skimmed his hand up her leg. His strong fingers worked their way over her pantaloons, caressing her skin. She moaned and wetness pooled between her thighs. Her core pulsed with need. She wanted him. To feel him inside her once more. To have his skin on her skin.

A tingling sensation started in her hips and grew until it raced up her spine. She found herself moving her hips against him as he settled his weight on her. He held her neck in his firm yet tender embrace, licking her while rubbing the other side of her throat with his thumb.

"Scarlet," he whispered. "Say my name." He squeezed her neck and sending a wisp of pain down her shoulders to her lower back. "Say it."

The pain mixed with the pleasure of his touch and she felt dangerously close to the edge. For all the control her aunt had taught her, she was like a lump of clay in his powerful hands.

He bit one of her taut buds through the thin fabric of her bodice.

"Jamen," she panted. She could barely breathe.

She moaned in delight and wove her fingers into his soft curls as he teased and tempted her through her dress. Every nerve ending of her body lit in a shower of sparks that left her sensitive to the touch. He looped a finger under the chain of her locket and pulled it slowly from between her breasts, kissing a trail back up to her mouth.

Distracted by the locket, images and emotions bombarded her. The pain, the loss, the emptiness. The screaming and fatigue.

He ran his fingers under the edge of her bloomers and pulled them down to her knees. Then he slid off his own breeches and their skin met. She sucked in a breath at the feel of his erection lying on her belly. His hand slid between her legs and suddenly the reality of what they were about to do hit her.

Jamen settled between her thighs and he press his hard length against her core.

Her heart raced. She couldn't do this. Not again. She couldn't risk it.

"Stop," she whispered.

He kissed a trail down her neck and pressed against her, coaxing her to let him enter. He pressed his manhood against her harder and a chill ran over her body. She tried to scoot out from under him.

"Jamen, stop!" she said.

He looked up, his eyes clouded with desire. "Am I hurting you?"

"No," she shook her head. Panic soured her mouth. "We can't. I mean, I can't."

His brows furrowed. "We can. It's fine. We're together, that's all that matters. Tomorrow we may not feel the same, but for tonight

117

we are together like we were meant to be." He dipped his head and his lips met hers again. He kissed her passionately and her mind swam. He positioned himself to enter her again.

No! This time she shoved him hard.

"Scarlet, I don't understand. I thought you wanted this." His eyes held fiery passion but his voice was soft.

"I did want this. I do want this, it's just…"

"What?" he asked. "Is it Edward?"

"No." She couldn't think straight. Memories collided with the desire racing through her body. "You don't have any covering."

"Lettie, I—"

"I can't risk getting pregnant again," she blurted.

His brow knit together and he his expression fell. "Again?" His voice was barely a whisper.

She took a deep breath. Tears flooded her eyes as he rolled on his side. All of her emotions collided, until she could hardly breathe. "When you broke it off. I was with child," she finally said.

A confused expression planted on his face. "But…You…I mean…"

"That night that I went to the tavern, I was going to tell you." Air whooshed out of her like a punch to the gut. She wished she could take back the words, but it was too late now. The burden she'd carried, the secret Aunt Liza had helped her hide. Now he knew.

He stared at the ceiling for a long time. "What happened?" he asked without looking at her.

The memories flooded back. "I was about three months gone

when I finally told my parents. My mother called a midwife immediately and told her to give me something to get rid of the child, but I refused to take it. Father said if I didn't they would disown me. So I went looking for you and then I packed a bag and ran. She took mercy on me and allowed me to stay with her through the pregnancy."

Sensations she hadn't expected rushed through her body. Her voice cracked as she spoke.

"When the time came, there was no one to call. No one she trusted to keep the secret. She and her maid Camille did what they could for me but in the end I labored too long. When the baby was born, she was dead."

Scarlet wrapped her arms around herself at the memories of holding her dark haired baby girl. The tiny body that had just days before, kicked her from inside, was bluish and lifeless. Tears streamed from her eyes and she hugged herself tighter.

"Aunt Liza buried the baby in the family cemetery. She tended to me through my months of grief, promising me that one day I would be wed and I'd have more children to replace the baby I lost. She tutored me in how to get a husband and how to keep him. But she was wrong. I think of our baby girl every day."

Scarlet pulled a chain from her neck. The locket that had been given to her by Jamen. He looked over at her as she opened it. Inside sat a small curl of hair, tied with a pink ribbon. She touched it tenderly and then showed them to him.

He stared at it for a long time. Raising his fingers he reached for the curl but stopped before he touched it. He jumped up suddenly and pulled on his breeches.

Scarlet wiped the tears from her eyes. "Where are you going?"

He moved about the room locating his tunic and pulling it on. Her blood pounded in her ears.

"Jamen," she pleaded. "Say something."

He didn't speak. Scarlet leapt from the bed and raced to him as he opened the door to go. She slammed her hand onto it, shutting it again.

"Jamen, don't do this. Don't shut me out. I'm sorry I didn't tell you sooner. It was wrong of me, but what choice did you give me? You left me!"

He turned to face her, his eyes full of pain. His jaw clenched several times.

Anger seeped through her at the sight. How could he be mad at her? This was his doing. He was the one who'd left her. Had he expected her to beg? To grovel?

"Go on then," she said, her voice flat and cold. "Run. It's what you do when a woman does more than just lie on her back for you, isn't it, Jamen?"

She let go of the door and crossed her arms over her chest. She'd been a fool to let him in again. She saw that now. He hadn't changed. Not one bit. She stepped away from him and he slipped out the door, closing it behind himself. She felt the door close as heavily as he'd closed her out of his heart.

Returning to her room she sat on her bed and stared at the door for a long time before crying herself to sleep.

CHAPTER TEN

The agony inside was enough to rip Jamen to pieces. He'd ruined Scarlet's life and he'd been the reason his own daughter was dead. Adrian was right. She was stronger than he'd given her credit for. To leave, disowned by her parents, and travel to live with an aunt she barely knew. To stay hidden because of the shame he'd brought upon her and then in the end to go through the pain of labor only to delivery a dead baby. It was more than he could take, and he'd only heard it.

Jamen stepped into the feasting hall not remembering where he was. He barely recalled leaving his room. The hall was quiet at the late hour. Only Angus, Redlynn's father, sat at a long table with a bottle of ale, staring into the large fire.

He looked up and waved Jamen over. "Join me for a drink?"

Jamen nodded and sat on the bench across from him.

"You look like you could use one." Angus pushed the bottle at Jamen who took several long swigs.

Jamen swallowed and sucked in a fiery breath. "I could use

more than one." Anger, grief and despair pulled him in so many directions that he wasn't sure which would kill him first.

"Female troubles?" Angus asked.

Jamen snorted. "Female troubles is an understatement beyond what I'm experiencing right now."

Angus drank deeply and stared into the fire. "Better to have female troubles, than to have no female to trouble you."

"Soon enough I'll have the latter. I'll let you know which is worse."

Jamen ran his finger over the surface of the table. He outlined her eyes, shaded in her nose and sketched the curve of her lips. Sights he'd dreamt about for the last three years. Etched into his memory now and forever. He blew out a sigh and rubbed his hand over the surface, wiping the image from his mind. He grabbed the bottle, trying to numb the thoughts in his head.

Angus sad countenance permeated the table. "Not having her is worse. You can take my word on that, son. At least now, even in the painful times, you have her near. You can smell her, feel her, see her. If only in her wrath, if only for a moment. When she's gone…" Angus turned away.

They sat in silence for several minutes. A baby. There'd been a *baby*. He'd left in an effort to avoid the very situation he'd ended up causing.

He'd been weak and a coward. If he'd been stronger, he would have married her. Had faith that his brothers would protect her. Made sure that he had contingencies in place in case anything happened. No wonder she hated him. He was a bastard.

"You should go to her," Angus said. "Tell her you love her. Make love to her. Let her know that she means the world to you. Give up everything you have to be with her. If she's your one, you'll be nothing without her."

Angus still stared into the fire.

"Is that what you did with Redlynn's mother?"

"No." Angus shook his head. "And I regret it every day of my life."

Jamen looked around the feasting hall. Everything spun slowly. Not quite drunk enough. He drained the rest of the bottle and sucked in a deep breath. The bottle tipped over as he tried to set it down. It rolled onto the floor with a clatter.

Angus stood and squeezed Jamen's shoulder. "I'll get us another."

*****

"Jamen…Jamen." A hand shook Jamen's shoulder. He jolted awake, to find himself still in the feasting hall. His head pounded from the ale. How many bottles had he finished off last night?

"Adrian." He wiped a spot of saliva from his chin. "I must have fallen asleep."

"Don't worry, all the men in Wolvenglen have spent at least a dozen nights at these tables. I wanted to let you know though that Lady Scarlet is anxious to leave."

Jamen was up on his feet; he rubbed the sleep from his eyes. "What?"

124

"She came to get Redlynn a half an hour ago. The sky is clear enough."

He stumbled and Adrian caught his arm. "Are you good to ride?"

Jamen straightened, blinked several times and then took a deep breath. "I'll be fine after I get something in my stomach."

"I'll have the women prepare some food."

Jamen nodded and headed for the stairs. "I thank you again for your hospitality."

Fifteen minutes later Jamen mounted his horse and trotted out the gate, ahead of Scarlet and Redlynn. Scarlet refused to even look at him. It stabbed him in the heart, but he understood. He wouldn't want to look at him either.

A thick rug of white snow covered the underbrush of the dense woods. The tall elder trees stood barren except for the dusting of white across their branches. Icy wind whipped white powder into his eyes. He rubbed at the flakes and blinked several times.

He hated winter. The bone freezing cold, the barren death of the land. But more than anything it was an external representation of how he felt inside on a daily basis. He pulled a biscuit from the food bag and ate it, refusing to give in to the desire for more alcohol.

Over the next several hours he glanced behind at Scarlet, hoping for a sign of affection from her as she rode next to Redlynn. Something, anything that would ease his burden. And every time he did, he cursed his selfish nature. She'd endured more than a woman had a right to, why should he be spared his moments of pain?

At noon they stopped near Volkzene to water the horses and rest. Redlynn and Scarlet dismounted.

"I have some ham and rolls in my pack. I'll water the horses while you eat," he said.

Scarlet looked pointedly away and Redlynn gave Jamen a tight smile and nod.

Redlynn pulled a blanket from her saddlebag and sat it on the ground. Jamen removed his satchel and handed it to Scarlet. She took it and for a moment he caught her eye. Her gaze was as dead as the fields of Westfall. A shudder of anguish sped to his heart.

He wanted to tell her he was sorry and to beg for her forgiveness. Why should she forgive him though? He couldn't forgive himself.

Instead he turned and headed for the creek.

*****

"Thank you again for allowing me to use a horse," said Scarlet.

Redlynn smiled. "Think nothing of it. We don't have much need for horses in Wolvenglen, so any exercise they can get is most welcome."

Scarlet divided up the meat and rolls and handed a portion to Redlynn who took the food with a smile. The anger that Jamen exuded from every pore was enough to make her want to punch him in the face. And though she'd tried to make small talk with Redlynn on the ride, her eyes had rarely left his broad frame. She memorized every crease of his cloak, every curl on his head. Even the number

126

of times he'd rubbed his neck. And all the while she'd hoped he would pull along side her and speak words that would ease the tension between them. But it was not to be.

"We'll be there soon, I'm sure," said Redlynn.

Scarlet bit into her sandwich, scanned the surrounding area and nodded. "Maybe another two hours," she said.

Voices pulled Scarlet's attention. Three men wrapped in thick clothing came around a bend and stopped walking. Redlynn stood and Scarlet followed suit. The groups stared at each other.

"Hello," Redlynn called.

The men whispered something and advanced; their stares giving Scarlet a sinking feeling. She glanced in the direction Jamen had gone but she couldn't see him.

"Hello yourself," one of the men called. "Nice day."

"Chilly," Redlynn said. "Where are you headed?"

The men reached the edge of the blanket.

"Just travelling. Seeing Fairelle." The lead man smiled, revealing stained, crooked teeth.

"Where have you been?" Redlynn asked.

"All over. Westfall, Volkzene, Draak Land."

"Draak Land?" said Scarlet. "That is quite south."

"A sight to behold. Dragon attacks happen almost daily there. We didn't stay long."

All three men looked from Scarlet to Redlynn. One of them scratched his crotch, making Scarlet wrinkle her nose.

"Where are your packs?" she asked, realizing they carried

nothing but the clothes on their backs.

The lead man laughed nervously and scratched his beard. "Oh, we don't have packs. They just weigh us down."

A gust of icy wind blew their direction whipping Scarlet's hair in her face.

In an instant Redlynn reached for her bow and knocked an arrow. "Get behind me."

Scarlet retreated. "What's wrong?"

"Now come on ladies, don't be like that," said the man.

"You should keep moving." Redlynn kept her eyes trained on the three men and pulled her bowstring till it creaked. "Trust me when I say, you don't want to pick a fight here today."

"Now what gave you the impression that we want to pick a fight?" The man crossed his arms.

"Because you smell of blood and fear."

*****

Jamen waited with the horses, sharing an apple with Brutin. The other two mares continued to drink from the stream where he'd kicked the ice away to reveal the flowing water underneath. He couldn't wait to get back to Sir Malcolm's and then to Gwyn Manor. Being near Scarlet was just too much for them both. With all the painful memories his presence stirred within her, he owed it to her to leave her be.

He held the apple core out to Brutin.

"JAMEN!"

He whipped around. The sound of Scarlet's terror sent a chill through him. Yanking his sword from his saddle he raced up the hill. He reached the road in time to hear Redlynn yell, "Run!"

Scarlet took off down the road a man following close behind. Two other men lunged at Redlynn, who spun out of the way and struck the first man in the face with her bow. She threw the bow to the ground and then reached into her boot and grabbed a large hunting knife.. Jamen rushed forward, knocking the second man to the ground with a blow from the pommel of his sword.

The first man got to his feet and spun around, his eyes wide in surprise. Jamen smashed him in the face with the flat of his sword. Blood burst from the man's nose.

"Go," Redlynn shouted, her eyes a golden glow. "I can handle this."

Jamen tore off after Scarlet. She'd left the road and ran into a frozen field of oatbern followed by a man. She turned back and lost her footing, and fell with a yelp. The man jumped on top of her. Anger mixed with a burst of energy, moving Jamen faster.

"Come on sweetie, don't be shy," the man said.

"Get off," she screamed. "Leave me be!" Scarlet scratched at the man's face, her legs flailing to kick him.

Jamen reached the man as he was pushing up Scarlet's dress. Rage coursed through him. His mind blocked out all sound and thought except for killing the attacker. He jumped on the man's back and pulled him from her. The man swung wildly trying to dislodge Jamen. Jamen had the man's head locked in his hands, trying to cut off his airway. A sudden sharp pain shot through Jamen's side, making his grip loosen. Both men toppled to the ground.

Jamen looked down. A knife protruded from his side. He yanked it out and tossed it away. Blood poured from his wound but he took no notice. All thought went to his desire to strangle the attacker. To feel the life escape him as he died.

Jamen got to his feet and the assailant rushed him, fists swinging. He dodged and punched the man in the gut. The attacker doubled over and Jamen tackled him. The man punched Jamen in the face but Jamen was unfazed. Blood and his Slayer instincts pumped through his limbs strengthening him.

He punched the man in the face over and over until his knuckles split and the man's eyes rolled into his head. Then he straddled the assailant and wrapped his hands around the man's throat. *Death.* The man deserved death for what he'd tried to do. How could a person be so foul?

Tighter and tighter he squeezed till the muscles in his hands cramped and his arms shook.

"Jamen! Stop, Jamen!" The calls came from far away. The pounding in his head muffling the cries.

His eyes trained on the man on the ground Jamen let his anger pour out of him. The scum had tried to rape Scarlet. How many other women had he hurt? Raped? Murdered? The man was no better than a daemon.

Jamen squeezed harder. The assailant's face turned blue. His eyes stared off, transfixed, his mouth open in a silent scream.

"Stop! You're killing him!"

The buzzing in Jamen's ears gave way to ringing. He looked up. Tears streamed down Scarlet's cheeks and her upper lip was wet. Terror etched her features. Scarlet!

He pried his fingers from the man's throat.

Everything moved slowly as he gazed around the barren field. He gulped in large bursts of air, his lung and throat burning like someone had lit coal inside him. He fell off the man and landed in a heap. Ice seeped through his cloak, chilling his skin.

The sound of Scarlet's muffled sobs broke through the ringing.

How had he gotten here? How had he become this man? She stared at the dead man, her eyes wide. He'd hurt her again. Her terror stricken expression struck him heavy as his father's broadsword. The look on her face shot through him. She was terrified of him.

Finally he'd done it. He'd shown her who he really was. There was no going back now.

CHAPTER ELEVEN

Scarlet's heart hammered like the pounding of a blacksmith's strike. Jamen had just killed a man with his bare hands. She stared at him, a stream of profanity and words coming out too fast for her to register what she said. He'd killed someone, to save her.

His wild eyes stared at her dangerously. He crouched on the ground staring as if he didn't even recognize her. She took several slow steps until she stood right in front of him. He blinked but didn't move. She knelt down until they were eye to eye. His body shook and his breathing was erratic.

She raised her hand and pushed the hair from his eyes. He stared at her for a moment more before reaching out and yanking her to him.

"Lettie," he whispered.

She wrapped him in her arms and held on.

"So many bad things. I've done so many things. Killed so many… Now you see. Now you understand. This is what I am now. I can't give you what you want, what you deserve."

132

"Shhhh… It's all right." Her words were as much a soothing balm to him as they were for herself. He'd killed someone. Her once shy, sweet artist who'd picked flowers for her and made her animals out of paper was a killer.

"Vampires. Male and female. I'd kill that man again and again for hurting you. I couldn't bear it if anything happened to you."

"Stop, Jamen. You're here with me and it's all going to be fine." She reached under his cloak and hugged him tighter. She needed the contact. As much as she should hold him for his sanity, she needed it too.

Warmth hit her arm and she pulled away. Blood smeared her skin.

"You're bleeding." Panic overtook her.

He felt inside his cloak. "It's not bad."

"Let me see." She pushed his cloak aside and tore his tunic. She gasped. A large deep wound wept heavily. His coloring was pale. "Jamen, this is bad."

"No, I'm fine. I heal fast." He staggered to his feet but fell.

"Jamen!" Scarlet looked around for Redlynn. Finally she lifted the hem of her dress and tore two pieces from the underskirt. She wadded the first into a ball and shoved it into his wound. The second she wrapped around his torso and tied off firmly.

His eyes fluttered open and closed several times but he barely even moved.

"…Damn you, Jamen Gwyn, if you die on me now you stubborn son of a— I'll never forgive you. Never…hear me? You stay here."

*****

Jamen startled awake to a piercing pain in his side.

"Ah," said Redlynn. "Decided to join us again did you?"

He scanned the area. His wet and frozen cloak clung to the icy ground of the oatbern field. The man he'd killed lay several feet away.

"What happened?" he croaked.

Redlynn tugged a needle and thread away from him.

"You lost a lot of blood. Good thing Scarlet stopped it when she did."

"How are you feeling?" Scarlet asked. Her eyes were puffy and swollen from crying and her skin held a swallow coloring. She glanced at what Redlynn was doing and then looked away again.

The way he'd acted after killing Scarlet's assaulter appalled him. He'd lost it in front of her. In more ways than one. He'd lost his temper and acted like a child afterward. He'd never reacted that way before. Then again, he'd never told anyone the feelings and thoughts he held deep inside. No one but her.

"I'm fine. We should get going." He made to sit up but Redlynn pushed him down.

"You can wait till I finish stitching you. This isn't my favorite thing to do, so the longer it takes the more likely I am to pass out or throw up. So stay still."

Jamen tried to hide the smile that threatened to take over. "You don't like blood?"

134

Redlynn's golden eyes flashed. "Don't ask."

He clamped his lips together and shook his head. It wasn't wise to argue or laugh at a woman who held a sharp instrument in her hands. Even a weapon as small as a needle.

He and Scarlet stared at each other, while Redlynn continued to sew. No words were said. Her skin continued to exude an ill pallor, but she stopped shaking and her breathing evened.

"Done," said Redlynn. She packed the needle and thread into a small case and then bandaged him again.

His spine ached and the stitched burned as he moved. "What happened with the other two men?"

"The one you knocked out on the road woke up and ran off. The other one and I had a nice long chat before he met his end."

"Find out anything useful?"

"He said something about being hired to kill a doctor and wife and to make it look like vampires did it."

He knew it. "Did he say who hired him or why?"

"All he said was that the doctor wouldn't go along with a plan to kill a Lady and so they got rid of him."

Jamen's gaze met Scarlet's. "Your aunt."

"But why would anyone want to kill her?" Scarlet said. "I don't understand."

Jamen staggered to his feet. His muscles compensated for the pain in his side. "It's common knowledge that she was known for... influencing many of the wealthy men of Fairelle in her day. Maybe one of them, or their wives, finally wanted revenge."

Scarlet's cheeks flushed with color. "How dare you speak of my aunt that way, you—"

Jamen rolled his eyes. "Truly Scarlet? You're going to adopt that indignant stance with me?"

"Lord Gwyn—"

"Oh don't Lord Gwyn me, woman. I'm right and you know it."

Scarlet snapped her lips together and stomped off toward the horses. Her curses floating back at him over her shoulder.

Redlynn snickered as she put her kit in her pack. "That isn't the best way to win her heart, Jamen,"

"Who said I wanted it?" He lied.

Redlynn stepped forward, leaned in close and sniffed his collar. "You do."

*****

Scarlet pulled her horse to a stop at the front of Sir Malcolm's estate and took a deep breath. It was time to face the piper. She took a moment to get her mind into the place her aunt had taught her. She smiled and was once again, Lady Scarlet. She hopped off her horse.

The door flew open and Edward ran out onto the gravel.

"Scarlet, where have you been? Are you all right? I was worried sick." He gathered her in his arms and then pushed her to arms length looking her over.

"I'm fine. We went to fetch the doctor for Aunt Eliza but... he was dead. So Lord Gwyn and I travelled to find a healer and got caught by last night's storm and had to stay the night."

"Yes," Edward said. "We came back because of the storm and

the servants said you and Lord Gwyn had gone to get help for your aunt."

Jamen and Redlynn stepped next to her and Edward.

"This is Qu—"

"Redlynn," Redlynn interrupted. "Just Redlynn." She stuck out her hand. Edward stared at Redlynn's face for several moments. Scarlet nudged Edward in the ribs.

"Excuse my staring, I've never seen eyes your color," he said.

Redlynn nodded and he grasped her hand and kissed it.

Her eyes met Scarlet's and she stifled a laugh by coughing. "I'm a healer and came to help Lady Eliza."

"Thank you," said Edward. "Wait. The doctor is dead?"

"Yes," said Scarlet. She glanced at Jamen. His pale face and sunken in eyes yelled that he needed to rest. "He and his wife were murdered."

"Murdered? By whom?"

"We don't know." A chilly wind whipped across Scarlet's face and she shivered.

"I'm sorry." Edward shook his head and wrapped a warm arm around her waist. "Come in. Please, come in and get warmed. Fredrick! Take care of the horses."

"I'll take care of Brutin," Jamen said.

"No." Scarlet stepped forward and realized she'd spoken too quickly. Her heart rate picked up. "You need to rest." She turned to Edward. "He's been injured."

"Injured?"

She wished she'd spoken with Jamen and Redlynn and agreed on how much they should say. She glanced at Jamen, but he just shook his head. "Well..." she stammered. "We were attacked on the road—"

Edward threw up his hands. "I think we better go inside where I can sit and hear the entire story from the beginning."

"Let me take Brutin." Scarlet said.

Jamen's face was pale and his expression impassive. She reached out and grabbed the reigns.

"We have a valet for that," said Edward.

She turned and smiled to Edward. "Brutin doesn't like most people, but he's gotten used to me over the past couple of days. I don't mind."

She turned back to Jamen. "Let me take him," she whispered.

He nodded. Clutching his side he moved off to the house. He hadn't uttered a word of complaint on the ride back, but she'd witnessed his shoulder slowly slump forward until she thought he might fall off. Now the waxy sheen to his skin made caterpillars crawl around inside her.

"I think maybe it's Lord Gwyn who needs a healer at the moment," said Edward.

Jamen didn't turn. "I just need to lie down for a bit and then I'll be good as new and out of your hair."

"I thought you were staying." Edward moved forward and caught Jamen under the arm, helping him into the house.

"No. I need to get to Gwyn Manor in light of recent

developments."

Redlynn, Jamen and Edward stepped into the house. Brutin nudged Scarlet in the shoulder. She rubbed his nose and sloshed toward the barn.

Jamen was leaving.

Scarlet sat at her aunt's bedside holding Liza's clammy hand. Redlynn hovered over her aunt, touching this and that and finally turned to Scarlet.

She blew out a long breath. "It's poison all right."

"You're sure?" asked Edward, his hand on Scarlet's shoulder.

"She shows the classic signs. The lips discolorations, sweats, vomiting, smell. All of it."

"But where? How?" he asked.

Redlynn's gaze locked on Scarlet. "When did she first grow ill?"

"About four nights ago. We'd been here a day and the night of the engagement celebration she began to feel poorly."

"What had she eaten that day?" Redlynn questioned.

Scarlet tried to remember. "Tea and sandwiches I think. Maybe some fruit. I'm not too sure."

"And they came from this house?"

"Now wait a minute," said Edward. "You can't possibly—"

"Be suggesting that some one here poisoned her? Yes, I absolutely am," said Redlynn.

"How dare you?" Edward moved away from Scarlet and stepped closer to Redlynn.

Redlynn chuckled. "Don't try to intimidate me. You have no idea who I am."

"Then tell me this," said Edward. "Why would someone in this house try to poison her?"

"That's not my problem. I am simply here to try and take care of Lady Eliza. I'll leave the tracking down of the would be murderer to the Gwyn brothers."

"Why would the Lords Gwyn track down the murders? That's for the local magistrate," said Edward.

"Can she be healed?" Scarlet cut in. Edward didn't need to know about Jamen and his brothers being Slayers.

Redlynn looked at Scarlet. "Healed? I don't rightly know. Can I get the poison out of her? Possibly. But Scarlet, your aunt is old, I don't know what long term affect this will have on her, or if she'll survive the process. I'll do my best but she should have seen a doctor days ago. You should prepare yourself for the worst."

A sob escaped Scarlet as she nodded and blinked back tears. Edward moved to her side.

"Don't worry, my dear. I will find out who did this and I will see them brought to justice. I promise you that no one in my household would have done this."

He stroked her cheek and Scarlet nodded and wiped her eyes. Edward kissed her on the top of the head and made for the door.

"I'll get to the bottom of this, and when I do, you'll have much to apologize for," he said to Redlynn.

She shrugged. "I doubt it."

Edward left without another word.

"Do you really think it was someone here?" asked Scarlet. She didn't dare believe it.

"Was she sick before you left?"

Scarlet didn't need to answer. She sighed and stared at her motionless aunt. *Please let her live, gods,* she prayed. *Liza is all the family I have left.*

"I need to get the toxins out of her," said Redlynn. "She needs to drink a mixture of herbs I'll make."

"I don't know that she can."

"Then we'll have to force her. Only you or I will prepare anything she eats or drinks from here on out. It's the only way we can be sure."

Scarlet's mind raced. "Eats or drinks…"

Redlynn looked up. "Who's been feeding her?"

"Her maid." Scarlet glanced around but Camille was missing. "She's been with her almost every moment since the first night."

"Then that's where you should start," Redlynn said. "Go get some hot water and I'll prepare the herbs."

Scarlet nodded. Apprehension bloomed within her. "I'm not sure Aunt Liza's maid had anything to do with it. The kitchen servants prepared the tea."

"Then maybe you should talk to them while you're down there. But be careful," Redlynn warned. "If anyone thinks you've discovered something, you could be in danger as well."

Redlynn removed several vials and pouches from her bag and

set them on a table. Pulling out a mortar and pestle she poured different herbs into the bowl and ground them up. Scarlet kissed her aunt's hand and then walked out.

*****

Jamen arose from the bed he'd previously refused to sleep in. The second leg of the ride back to Westfall had been almost excruciating. He was pretty sure that if it hadn't been for his extra healing abilities and Redlynn stitching him up, he'd have died in that frozen field. In an effort to not cause Scarlet any further concern he'd done his best to show no weakness. He all but screamed weakness now by napping on the too soft, too pretty bed.

He grimaced and lifted his shirt. Blood had seeped through the bandages, but not enough to become worrisome. He ran his tongue over the roof of his mouth. It clung like tar.

He made his way to the water pitcher and hefted it, but there was not a drop inside. Cursing, he ambled to the door, pulled it open and made his way toward the kitchen.

He was half way down the stairs when Scarlet's voice floated up to meet him.

"I know it was one of you! Tell me who made the tea!"

He hurried down and came to a halt in the doorway. Scarlet brandished a knife and all of the kitchen servants were backed into a corner.

"One of you prepared the water and the tea for my Aunt, now tell me who it was!" she said.

"Scarlet." Jamen took several steps forward. She spun around, the knife outstretched. Jamen raised his hands and stepped away.

"Poison," she said. "In the tea."

Her face was haggard and there were deep circles under her eyes. "Scarlet," he said, keeping his voice even. "Give me the knife."

"One of them poisoned her, Jamen, and I want to know why." She looked half crazed with fatigue. How much sleep had she been getting?

He lowered his voice and spoke to her as he used to when it was just the two of them alone. "I know and we will, but you have to put the knife down."

Her expression was one of confusion. After all she'd lost, the thought of losing her aunt had her dangerously close to cracking. It was written all over her.

He took a step closer. Her shoulders sagged and he moved to her in one large step and pried the knife from her grip. A pain shot up his side as a stitch popped from the sudden movement.

"They tried to kill her," she whispered. "If you hadn't been here to help…"

He wanted to hold her, to kiss her and make everything better.

He sat Scarlet in a chair at the far end of the preparation table and then turned and walked back to the servants.

"You know who I am?"

They nodded.

"Tell me then, as Lord of these lands. Tell me who prepared the tea for Lady Scarlet's aunt."

The group looked at each other. Finally the cook stepped

forward.

"It was Fredrick, M'lord."

Jamen sucked in a deep breath. "Fredrick the manservant?"

The cook nodded.

"Does he usually make tea?"

"No, M'lord. This is the first I've seen of it. He and Camille made the tea together."

"Where is he?" Jamen asked.

The servants looked at each other again.

"I'm not sure," the cook said. "He left in a hurry a few moments ago with Camille. The two have spent every spare moment together since Lady Scarlet arrived."

Jamen waved off the servants and sat with Scarlet, out of earshot. "It seems Fredrick is the culprit, or the scapegoat," he said.

"And Camille? But why would she do such a thing?"

"That is a question we will need to ask once we find them," said Jamen. "It seems though that there is most likely a reasonable answer to that question."

"Which is?"

Jamen raised his eyebrows and stared at her.

She leaned in close. "Not Edward," she said in a lowered voice.

"I'd see him hanged if he hurt you."

Her eyes narrowed and she pursed her lips. "It wasn't Edward. He's gentle and kind. He'd never do a thing to hurt me or anyone else. You've met him. Do you think he is really capable of doing something like that? Besides. He doesn't have the wits to pull something like that off."

The desire to hold her and be held by her was all consuming. He reached across the table to where her hand sat but then pulled it away.

"I'm just asking. You know I have to search out every possibility. But you're right. I don't think he possesses the aptitude to put together such an elaborate plan." His mind raced. "There might be someone else who could though."

"Who?"

The cook came over and they stopped talking. She set two mugs of wine between them.

"The hot water is ready for you to take up," said the cook.

Jamen nodded in thanks and downed his drink. Scarlet sipped hers and then rose.

"I need to get some hot water to Redlynn," Scarlet said.

Jamen patted her hand. "You should lie down. It's been a rough couple of days. I'll take the water up."

Scarlet's eyes drifted to where his hand sat. She covered his hand with hers and entwined their fingers, making his heart gallop. He needed to get away before he did something they would both regret at this point.

He pulled his hand back. "Rest. I'll be sure to wake you if anything happens with your aunt or we find Fredrick and Camille."

Scarlet gave him a mild smile and left without another word. Her delicate hips swished as she ascended the stairs. He reached over and downed her cup of wine.

Jamen knocked on the door and then entered Liza's room. Redlynn waited by the bed, dabbing Liza's forehead with a wet cloth.

"I have the water."

"Good," she said. We'll need to try and get it down her throat. She isn't going to like it I'm afraid."

"What do you need from me?"

"Hold her mouth open."

Jamen handed the pot to Redlynn and she poured her herbs in. He walked to Lady Eliza's side and sat on the bed.

"Lady Eliza?" he shook her shoulder.

She moaned but didn't open her eyes.

Jamen leaned in close. "Lady Eliza, you've been poisoned. We need you to drink this tea or you won't live the night I'm afraid. You must drink it. Scarlet needs you."

Her eyes fluttered open momentarily.

"Can you swallow?"

Lady Eliza opened her mouth. Redlynn moved to the bed and blew on the tea. She nodded to Jamen and he slipped his palm under Lady Eliza's head and tilted it back. Redlynn poured the liquid into Lady Eliza's mouth and she swallowed once but then she sucked in an enormous breath and cried out.

"Hold her!" Redlynn commanded.

Jamen gripped the older woman's neck and held her mouth open. Redlynn poured more in. Lady Eliza coughed and choked but it went down. Streams of liquid dripped out of the corners of her mouth, staining her chemise. Redlynn poured until the cup was empty.

"What was in that?" asked Jamen.

"Herbs to burn out the poison."

"She's in pain." Jamen removed his hand and put a rag on her forehead.

"Not as much as she will be in a few hours." Redlynn set the cup on the table and then dipped several strips of cloth in the liquid left in the pot. She walked back and opened Lady Eliza's chemise. Jamen turned away as she set the strips on Lady Eliza's chest.

When she'd finished she locked eyes with Jamen. "Let me see your wound."

"I'm fine." He stood and moved away.

"We should change the bandage at least."

He wanted to protest but didn't.

He stared at the wall while Redlynn checked and rebandaged his wound.

"You should've died from that you know."

"I do."

"Good thing you're a Slayer." Her eyes met his.

"Yeah," he said. "Good thing." What a strange turn of fate that the one thing that had allowed him to save Scarlet from her attacker was the one thing that kept them apart.

"Why aren't you fighting for her?" Redlynn asked.

Jamen's brows knit. "Excuse me?"

"You love her and she clearly loves you, yet you aren't fighting for her. You're letting her marry another. *Another* who might be an attempted murderer."

"Edward didn't do this. Of that I'm certain."

"You didn't answer my question." Redlynn moved back to Lady Eliza and dabbed her again.

"Sometimes two people have so much pain between them that the only way for them to find happiness is to move on." His stomach soured at the thought.

Redlynn nodded. "You keep telling yourself that, Jamen Gwyn, but I saw how she was when you passed out and she thought you were going to die. There was nothing about her affection that said she wanted to move on."

Jamen rubbed his face and ran his fingers through his hair. "You don't understand. The things I've done…what I've put her through… Being a Slayer. Everything about me causes her pain and puts her in danger. She deserves better than that. Edward can give her a normal life. A stable life."

Redlynn stopped dabbing and turned to face him. "I went into Wolvenglen Forest to kill the King of the Weres. To kill Adrian. He hid from me the fact that he was a wolf and what I was. His kinsmen killed my best friend and allowed vampires to feed off children I was duty bound to protect. I'd say that we had a few things between us when we mated. But we worked through them, together. It's not the things you've done to hurt her that matter, Jamen. It's the things you do now to make amends."

She didn't understand. How do you make amends for the death of a child? An image of the small dark curl of hair Scarlet still held in her locket tugged at Jamen's heart. *His* daughter. He'd had a daughter and he didn't even know her name.

"You should go to her," said Redlynn. "Tell her you're sorry. Make love to her, make her yours."

Jamen laughed. "Angus said something very similar in Wolvenglen."

"My father is a wise man."

Jamen sat on the small settee in a corner of the room and relaxed into it. He watched Redlynn dab at Lady Eliza and tend to her with a compassion that reminded him of his sister Snow.

After several minutes his eyelids drooped and he gave in to slumber.

"Jamen?" Redlynn shook his shoulder. "I think you should go to your room. You'll be more comfortable there."

"How long have I been asleep?" He stretched his legs.

"About an hour."

"Has Scarlet been by?"

"No she's still resting as well. I'll come get you if there is any change," Redlynn said.

He got to his feet, walked to the door and stepped out into the hall. He looked toward Scarlet's room.

Maybe it was possible. Maybe if he went to her now she would forgive him. If there was any shred of hope—

No. He needed to let her move on. His boots clunked on the floor as he made his way back toward his room. He passed Scarlet's door and noticed it was ajar. He stopped and listened.

"I'm so sorry, Scarlet. Camille and Fredrick were found just outside Westfall. They were dead when we got there. It looked like they'd taken poison. Your maid clutched a note however. She said that she tried to kill your aunt because Lady Eliza was a harlot who ruined men and she had to be stopped."

"But that doesn't make any sense. My aunt was but nice and fair to Camille."

"I'm sorry, my dear. That's all I know."

"But—"

"Scarlet, this I know for sure. I will never let anything happen to you. Forever."

"You can't say that," she said. "No one knows what forever holds."

"That is true, but I will spend my life doing everything I can to make sure you are happy and safe. I love you, Scarlet. I've loved you since the first moment I laid eyes on you. The day you said you'd be my bride was the happiest of my life."

Jamen's heart shredded. He backed away from the door. He didn't want to hear her reply. The pain in his soul was already caving in on him.

CHAPTER TWELVE

Jamen slept the rest of the day. At dinner time Edward came to see him bringing him more food than he could eat in a week and pledging fealty to the Gwyn family. Edward begged for Jamen to believe that they had nothing to do with the poisoning of Lady Eliza.

Jamen said that he would bring the information to his brothers to make a decision. As Lords of Westfall they had the final say. Edward thanked him for his graciousness and then left.

He ate on the bed in silence, making the plethora of pillows prop him and his platter up. A knock pulled him from his food. He crossed to the door and opened it wide. Redlynn stared at him. She swallowed hard and then shook her head.

"I did what I could, but it was too late."

Jamen cursed and rubbed his face with his hands. "Does Scarlet know?"

"I thought it best if it came from you."

This was the last thing he wanted to do.

"I can prepare the body if you'd like."

Jamen waved his hand. "No, no. I'll see that it's done. Gather your things and I'll get you to the Wolvenglen Forest."

"You're going home too." It wasn't a question.

"She's better off here."

"I tend not to meddle in other's decisions, but I tell you this now Jamen, you are wrong. Some people were meant to be together."

Jamen looked toward Scarlet's door. "Even if you're right, it's too late. I've done everything in my power to push her into Edward's arms. He is a good man and he really cares about her. How could I do that to them both? I've done a lot of things to bring shame upon my family, I can't do this as well."

"What about you Jamen? You care about everyone else but yourself. When are you going to do something that makes you happy?"

Jamen shrugged. "I've been unhappy for so long, I don't know that I even remember how."

Redlynn squeezed his shoulder. "You do. I've seen it in your eyes when you look at her."

She walked back the way she came and closed the door to Eliza's room with a click. Jamen took several deep breaths and headed for Scarlet's room. He stood outside the door for several minutes without moving. He and Scarlet had been meant for each other once upon a time. But that future had passed. She deserved to be happy.

He swallowed and knocked. A shuffle of footsteps sounded

152

from the other side. The door opened and her bright green eyes peered out at him.

"Lord Gwyn, can I help you?"

Jamen's tongue clung to the roof of his mouth. He didn't have the words.

Her brows furrowed. "Lord Gwyn?"

He reached out and stroked her cheek. His arms trembled from the desire to hold her. To keep this pain from her. If he could have born it for her, he would.

She pulled away. "Jamen, we can't—"

He dropped his hand. "Lettie, I'm sorry. Redlynn did all she could, but the poison was too strong."

Scarlet searched his face. "No. No, you said Redlynn could heal her. Redlynn said the herbs would work."

"Lettie—" He reached for her, but she pushed past him and ran to her aunt's room. "Lettie!" he called after her. "Don't."

****

Scarlet burst through the doors to her aunt's room, the scent of herbs filled the stuffy air. Redlynn looked up from packing her bag. Scarlet's mind reeled as she turned to her aunt. Aunt Liza's ashen skin was almost blue. The bed sheet had been pulled up to her chin.

"Lady Scarlet," said Redlynn.

She rushed to the bed and sat at her aunt's side. Her insides twisted into a knot and her limbs shook like someone had struck her with lightning.

"Aunt Liza. Aunt Liza wake up." Tears blurred her vision and

153

she sobbed once. "Aunt Liza?" Scarlet shook her aunt's shoulder and her head lolled to one side.

"Lettie." Jamen's arms surrounded her. "Lettie, come away."

"No." She pushed at him. "Aunt Liza, wake up! I need you."

"Lettie." Jamen was stronger. He lifted her from the bed pulling her close.

She screamed and beat on his chest. "Let me go! Let go, Jamen."

He held her and spoke soothing words in her ear but she couldn't make anything out from the pounding of blood in her head.

"Make her wake up," she cried. "Make her wake up." She clung to him. How could this be happening? The woman who'd loved her and helped her and taken her in, was dead. Now she had no one.

"What's happening?" Edward's voice floated in from the doorway.

Jamen's grip disappeared and Scarlet looked up through her flurry of tears.

"Lady Eliza is dead," said Jamen. "Lady Scarlet needs you."

No! I need you! She wanted to scream. Jamen stepped away and Edward took his place, enveloping Scarlet and stroking her hair. Over his shoulder Scarlet stared at Jamen.

His expression held sadness that she felt in her soul. She needed him. Why couldn't he see that? Why didn't he try? He just gave her to Edward. Moments ago he'd held her and soothed her the way he had when her pet cat had been struck by a carriage. He had to care.

"I will be escorting Redlynn to… her home," Jamen said. "I'll see to it that the undertaker is summoned when I go."

"Go?" said Edward.

"I know the timing is poor," said Jamen. "But I must. Redlynn needs to return home, and I…" He locked eyes with Scarlet. "I need to get word to my brothers of Lady Eliza's passing."

"We're to be celebrating our wedding in a few days, but now it seems we shall be planning a funeral instead," said Edward.

"My condolences to you both," Jamen bowed to Scarlet.

She ached to run to him, to beg him to stay. But how could she when it was so obvious that he wanted to leave.

"If there is anything you need, please, don't hesitate to let me know," said Jamen.

"Thank you, Lord Gwyn." Scarlet's throat burned. Every word she spoke tasted bitter and repugnant. "You are too kind."

He nodded and then turned to Redlynn. "I'll be ready within the half hour."

"I'll get the horses." Redlynn fashioned her red cloak about her and grabbed her bag. She turned to Scarlet. "I am truly sorry for your loss Lady Scarlet."

Both Jamen and Redlynn nodded and then walked out. Scarlet's heart broke with Jamen's every step away from her.

"Come," said Edward. "Let's get you to your room and get you a cup of tea."

"No." She pushed away from him. "I never want another cup of tea in my life."

Edward's brows furrowed and then he nodded. "Whatever you

wish, my dear."

CHAPTER THIRTEEN

Jamen pulled to the stable behind Gwyn Manor and unsaddled Brutin. After taking Redlynn to the edge of Wolvenglen Forest he'd headed home. He couldn't take seeing Scarlet with Edward. Though he'd come to accept that Edward was a good man and would be good to Scarlet, it was too painful to witness her with someone else. Especially now.

He opened the stable door and walked Brutin to his stall. Brutin reared back and pulled from Jamen's grasp.

"Damned animal," Jamen cursed.

Brutin pushed Jamen aside and trotted to the stall after his. A smaller black mare popped her nose out, surprising Jamen. Brutin and the mare rubbed necks and Jamen smiled. His gaze travelled out the door toward the manor house. He wasn't alone.

He threw the saddle over one of the other stalls and went to the mare and rubbed her nose. "Hello, Rulian, where did you come from? Where's Erik?"

Jamen grabbed Brutin's reins and got him settled into his own stall and then headed for the house.

He pushed open the door to the solar to find Erik sitting at the table entertaining Belle's daughter Chloe.

"Uncle Jamen!" Chloe cried from the table. She ran and hugged him around the legs.

The smell of cooking meat wafted from the kitchen. In the corner of the solar stood a large evergreen decorated with beautiful colored glass. A fire warmed him from the fireplace.

Erik smiled. "I heard you might need some company." He took a deep swig from his mug of ale.

Jamen crouched down and hugged Chloe. Coming home to find Erik there made his chest squeeze. And the feel of Chloe's small arms hit him in a place he'd never known he had before.

"You said you'd dance with me," she pouted.

"Indeed I did. And I'm sorry about that. Next time. I promise." He grabbed one of Chloe's blond curls and pulled on it lightly. The silky feel made him shudder. He wondered if that was how their daughter's hair would have felt.

Belle entered carrying a large platter of food. She smiled. "I hope you don't mind that I did some decorating."

"Not at all, but how did you get in?"

Belle laughed. "You Gwyn's are nothing if not creatures of habit. I knew where Snow's key was in the aviary. I wasn't expecting you for a few more days so I didn't have time to finish unfortunately."

"It's just right," said Jamen. "Thank you."

She smiled.

"Where's Klaus?"

Belle's smile fell. "He had some business to attend to, so we decided it was the perfect time to come visit, didn't we Chloe?"

Chloe nodded.

Jamen understood that it was best if he waited till Chloe was out of earshot before asking more questions.

"Come," said Belle. "Eat. I made enough for everyone."

Jamen hefted Chloe and sat with her in a chair at the table. He stared at the back of Chloe's head. His gut twisted like someone was strangling him from the inside.

"Are you all right?" asked Erik.

Jamen sniffed and then cleared his throat. "Yeah, sure."

Erik leaned over and laid his hand on Jamen's shoulder. "I'm sorry about Scarlet."

Jamen bit his cheek and watched Chloe pile her plate high with chicken and vegetables and rolls.

"Hey. You gonna eat all that?" He laughed.

"It's for you," she said.

"For me?"

"Next one is for Uncle Ewik. You need it."

"Why do you say that?" asked Erik.

"Because you're vampire kiwers and need to be stwong."

Erik and Jamen exchanged a look.

"Sweetie, who told you that?" asked Jamen.

"No one. I see it," said Chloe. "You both glow on the outside."

Again Erik and Jamen stared at each other.

"Hey, Chloe," said Erik. "Can you go get Uncle Jamen a cup from the kitchen?"

"Sure." Chloe smiled and ran off.

Jamen tracked her tiny steps as she went. "What the hell was that?"

"She may be a seer," said Erik. "Or a mage."

"But all the way up here? Both races come from the south. And Klaus is no seer or mage."

"Could come from Belle's side."

Chloe toddled in followed by Belle. They set down drinks and each took a seat. The group held hands and said thanks to the gods before eating. It was a strange ritual that hadn't happened in Gwyn Manor since the death of his mother.

"Thank you for coming," Jamen said. "The manor wouldn't be the same for Yuletide Festivus with only me in it to celebrate."

Erik nodded his shaggy blond head and flashed the same smile their father used to own. "That's what family is for."

The next several days passed in a blur of loneliness and heartbreak. As Scarlet's wedding day loomed ever closer Jamen sank deeper into melancholy than he was used to. The only reason he'd kept from drinking himself into a stupor was Belle and Chloe.

Belle had admitted to him and Erik of Klaus' infidelities and decided she needed some time apart. With nowhere else to go, she'd come to Gwyn Manor. The only place she'd ever felt safe. Jamen told her of Snow and the family secret they'd been keeping for the past several years.

Belle agreed to stay on and help cook at the Manor in exchange for food and lodging for both her and Chloe. The sweet spirit that Chloe brought to the house both comforted and pained Jamen.

He and Erik had spent every evening talking. Something Jamen couldn't remember having done with anyone other than Scarlet. It eased his mind to tell his older brother what had happened with Scarlet, but not his heart. Jamen's ached worse than ever for her.

The eve before Yuletide Festivus he sat with Erik drinking wassail in the solar as Belle tucked Chloe into bed in Snow's old room.

The small room was the only part of the large manor that felt like home. So many of his memories from the past three years had been made in that room.

"Do you really think she'll marry Edward?" Erik asked.

Jamen twirled the emerald ring on his pinky finger. "I hope she does," he lied.

"You don't mean that."

"No. I don't. But I do want her to find happiness and peace. She won't find that with me."

"You didn't break her, Jamen."

"What I put her through. The baby..."

Erik shook his head and squeezed Jamen's hand. "That wasn't your fault, brother."

Jamen met his eye. "Wasn't it? I couldn't keep my breeches tied and because of it—"

"We all make mistakes. Me, Flint, Kellan. All of us."

Jamen drained his cup. "It doesn't matter." He stood and walked to the kitchen, set his cup in the wash basin and slumped back to the solar. "I'm going to bed."

A soft knock sounded on the solar door. Jamen looked at the clock. It was late.

Erik shrugged. "Open it."

Jamen crossed to the door and pulled it open. In the darkness stood a woman in a long chartreuse cloak. Her breath caused small puffs of white in front of him. She pulled back her hood revealing emerald green eyes.

Scarlet. He stared at her unable to believe that she was actually there. He stopped himself from grabbing on to her and yanking her to him.

"May I come in?" She raised her eyebrows.

"Of course." He pulled the door open wider and she stepped in. He scanned outside but there was no one in sight. A horse stood tied to the stable door. Jamen closed the door and turned to see Erik embrace Scarlet tightly.

"How are you? I'm sorry to hear of your aunt's passing."

Scarlet nodded. "Thank you, Erik."

"We will find out who did this to her. One way or another." Erik's voice held the tone of a Lord.

"Again, I thank you. That's the reason I've come. I don't believe that my aunt's maid and Fredrick acted alone. I believe someone

162

forced them to kill my aunt."

"Do you have any proof?" asked Jamen. His fingers itched to hold her. He folded his arms over his chest and clenched his fists.

She turned to him. The circles under her eyes were deep, but she still looked radiant in the firelight glow.

"No. Not proof per say."

"Then what?" asked Erik.

She licked her lips. "I overheard Edward's older brother Lyden speaking to some friends. He mentioned that my aunt had been worth a lot of money and that now the money was mine and would soon be Edward's. He said that it was blood money and he was going to be used to help take down the Gwyn's and put Sir Malcolm in your place."

Erik's posture stiffened. "Where was this?"

"At Edward's house. The men were drinking and it was late, but I couldn't sleep so I'd gone for a walk and passed the solar where I heard them."

"Did anyone see you?" The hairs prickled on Jamen's arms.

"I don't think so."

"I overheard the servants talking in the kitchen last week," said Jamen. "They were complaining that they hadn't been paid."

"Then it is possible that Lyden and Malcolm killed Lady Eliza for her money," said Erik.

Jamen looked at Scarlet and then to Erik. "It's too dangerous for Scarlet to go back. If they find out she's been here, they may get the idea that she overheard."

"I agree," said Erik. "You should stay here until we have this sorted out."

"And how long will that be?" she asked. "My aunt's funeral is the day after tomorrow. I was only able to sneak out tonight because Sir Malcolm is having a large party and I told them I didn't feel up to entertaining. They believe I'm sleeping, but in the morning they'll know I am gone."

"Then you shall stay here with us for Yuletide tomorrow and then we'll escort you to your aunt's funeral," said Erik.

A stricken expression came over her. "I can't. I must get back. I just wanted to warn you."

"I'll go with you," Jamen offered. "Erik's right. If they figure out what you heard, you could be in danger."

"They won't hurt me. Edward wouldn't let them." She turned for the door. Jamen grabbed her hand and she stopped.

"I'll leave you two alone." Erik set his cup on the table and left, closing the solar door behind him.

Sorrow clouded Scarlet's eyes.

He'd take her to her aunt's estate. Or somewhere else, but not to Edward. Not now. Edward may not be involved, but his father and brother couldn't be trusted.

But she'd come here. She could have waited till he'd come to the funeral but she hadn't.

"Why did you come?" He entwined his fingers with hers and backed her into the door. Her eyes widened.

"I told you, I came to warn you and to get your help." She

164

swallowed hard.

He moved closer until his body was almost touching hers. The sparks that jumped between them were magnetic. She moved and his body followed. It was as it had always been between them. A connection that couldn't be broken.

He reached out and brushed a red hair from her face.

"You could have sent a letter, or waited till I'd come for the wedding."

Her eye flicked sideways and then back to his face. "I was afraid it might be intercepted... and I didn't want to..." She sucked in a raspy breath.

He leaned in close, the smell of rosewater wafted off of her making his arousal grow. He should stop. He bent his head and rested his forehead on hers. "Why did you come?"

"I missed you," she whispered. Her chin quivered. "I needed you and you left me."

"You have Edward."

She was silent for a long time. "I don't want Edward."

"You've seen my world, what I do, who I am. I'm not good enough for you, Lettie. You deserve better. You need to stay away, stay safe."

"You keep saying that. Stay away, stay safe, but I've seen your world, my world. Fairelle. I've seen what you do and what you go through for everyone. How is staying away safer for me? If you hadn't been there I'd have been raped or worse by that attacker."

She reached up and put her hands on either side of his face.

They locked eyes and his heart raced in his chest. "I see you, Jamen. I see who you are and I'm still here."

He swooped down and crushed her mouth with his. She wrapped her arms around his neck and pulled his body into hers. This is what he'd wanted for the last three years, and he wasn't going to second guess it. This time, she would be his.

*****

Scarlet reveled in the feel of Jamen's hard body against hers. She'd fought the urge to run to him, but after days of grief with no one but Edward to talk to, she given in. She didn't want Edward, she wanted Jamen. It had always been Jamen and always would be.

His hand roamed under her cloak. Undoing the clasp she shrugged it off her shoulders and it fell to the ground. He kissed down her neck, his fingers rubbing the sensitive peaks of her breasts. She moaned his name and reached for the tie on his breeches. She didn't care anymore. Not about Edward, not about the past, none of it. Her aunt was dead and she had no one to answer to anymore except her heart. And her heart wanted him.

She slid his breeches to the ground and he ran his hands under her dress and up her thighs. Scarlet quivered with delight as he slid off her pantaloons. Then his mouth claimed hers again and she held her skirts at her waist. He pressed into her and stopped.

"Are you sure?" he asked.

A wave of anxiety washed through her but was replaced by need. She gripped his hard length and guided it toward her core. He sucked in a breath and pounded on the wood beside her head.

"Lettie." His voice was horse and strained. "I don't know how long I can hold out."

She kissed him again and he entered her, grabbing at her rear he hefted her off her feet. She wrapped her legs around his waist as he thrust deep inside her. The feel of him sending a wave of chills over her skin. She cried out and dug her nails into his skin.

He broke their kiss. "Am I hurting you?" His eyes were full of love and concern.

She held his gaze. "More."

A smile played on his lips as he turned and laid her gently on the rug in front of the fireplace. Poised above her he kissed her as he lifted her leg over his shoulder and thrust deeper. Scarlet gasped at the sensation and held on to his hips as he continued to thrust and their bodies joined. Her mind floated away in a sea of ecstasy. How long she'd waited to be with him again. To feel him inside her. Filling her, spilling into her. He was hers. eH

Jamen's muscles bunched beneath her touch. His breathing quickened and he tensed. He called her name over and over as he reached climax. Scarlet smiled and a tear leaked from her eye.

When he finished their eyes locked. He released her leg and dropped down on top of her, holding her face with his hands. They lay on the floor, bodies joined, kissing and touching and basking in the feel of each other.

Finally he broke the silence. "Marry me, Scarlet. I know I don't deserve you and you have no reason to want me, but I love you. I've always loved you and no other. I can't promise you life will be easy, but I can promise that I will love you till the day I die. I don't know how many years—"

"Jamen, shut up." She grabbed his face in her hands and kissed him. "Yes, yes, a million times yes. If I had you for only tonight, I would still say yes."

He balanced on his elbows and pulled the emerald ring from his pinky. He removed the ring Edward had given her and replaced their original engagement ring.

Tears flowed from her eyes and he kissed them away.

"I'll never leave you again, Lettie. Only death can part us now."

She beamed up at him, her heart so full she thought she might burst. All that they'd been through, all of the pain, it only made their bond that much stronger. Their love that much deeper.

"Stay with me tonight," he said.

"Forever," she replied.

Jamen carried Scarlet from the solar up to his bedroom. They made love till late into the night and then she slept while he held her close. He was too scared to close his eyes for fear that he'd find it had all been a dream.

In the morning the sound of Yuletide songs awoke them.

"Happy Yuletide," he said. He pulled her naked body on top of his and kissed her deep and long.

"The best one yet," she replied.

"Hey, Jamen—" The door opened and Erik poked his head in the room. Scarlet ducked under the covers and Jamen laughed. "Oh, sorry." Erik's face reddened. "Uh…Chloe is opening a few presents if you... and Scarlet want to join us."

"We'll be down in a minute," said Jamen.

Erik mouthed sorry, but then smiled at Jamen. After he closed the door Jamen ducked under the covers. Scarlet's red hair stuck out in every direction but her face glowed. He pulled her close and slung her knee over his hip.

"I have nothing to give you for Yuletide," he said. She kissed him and wrapped her hands around his growing arousal. He moaned and closed his eyes.

"Everything I want is right here."

He sucked in a sharp breath as she stroked him with her soft fingers. His mind stopped working as pleasure spread from his groin down his legs, making his limbs tingle.

"But what can I give you?" she mused.

He tried to concentrate on something other than the feel of her touch. He trailed a finger down her throat and between her breasts to where the locket dangled.

"Tell me just one thing," he said.

"Anything." She kissed his collarbone and swirled her tongue up the side of his throat.

"What's her name? The name of our daughter?"

Scarlet stopped moving. She blinked several times and then licked her lips. "Cosette."

"Little thing," he said.

Scarlet peered at him, and chewed the inside of her cheek.

"I want to move her. Bring her here. Bury her with my family.

Our family. To be near us and to give her a proper marker."

Scarlet's eyes teared and she nodded vigorously. "I'd like that very much."

He cradled her face in his palms. "No more do you need to hide who you are, Lettie. You can hold your head high for what you have been through. For who you are. You don't need my name. You have your own. Your own money and you can stand on your own. You've proven that."

"I don't want the money or the name, I just want you. That's all I've ever wanted. I don't care what people whisper when I walk by, as long as they are whispering about me as your wife."

Jamen smiled. "Then let's get Erik."

CHAPTER FOURTEEN

Jamen awoke early the following morning and proceeded with Erik to Sir Malcolm's house. He left Scarlet with Belle and Chloe to get ready for the funeral.

They rode at a quick pace, getting to the manor just as Father Ohana arrived.

"I must leave when the funeral is done," said Erik. "I need to get to Tanah Darah and speak with Gerall, Hass and Ian. Can you hold down the Manor House till we return?"

"Of course," Jamen replied. "Though I wish Flint was with us." Flint was the strongest and fiercest of them all. With him at Gwyn Manor any plotting against his family was sure to crumble.

"I agree."

Jamen brought his horse to a halt and dismounted. They greeted Father Ohana and then headed for the front door. Jamen's stomach soured at what he was to do.

A servant answered the door and showed them into a sitting room to the left. A large Yuletide tree, burdened with baubles and trinkets glistened in the corner. Several unwrapped boxes sat sadly under the tree. He wondered if they were for Scarlet and he was struck with a pang of guilt.

Sir Malcolm and Edward entered and stopped short upon seeing Erik.

"Lord Gwyn," said Sir Malcolm. "I didn't know you were in Westfall."

"I am never far from Westfall," Erik replied. He stood tall and proud, commanding respect the way their father had.

"It is good that you are here," said Edward. "There have been several murders and now Lady Scarlet has gone missing."

"They say vampires are responsible for at least two of the deaths," said Sir Malcolm. "But as vampires don't exist, that is impossible. Isn't it?"

"Do they exist?" Erik twirled their father's ring on his hand. "Tell me, Sir Malcolm, do you believe there are vampires?"

"Well, I'm sure I do not know. I've not seen, nor heard of any, I'm sure. But as Lord of the land, if anyone would know about such thing, it would be you and I'm sure if there were such a threat, you would tell us," said Sir Malcolm.

Jamen got an uneasy feeling. Sir Malcolm's words were more of an accusation than mere innocent gossip.

"And who says it was vampires?" asked Jamen.

"Why everyone," answered Edward. "The doctor and his wife were found by several townsfolk and they all saw the wounds, the blood. And the word 'vampire' scrawled on the floor."

"Indeed," said Erik.

"But I am more concerned with the disappearance of Lady Scarlet," continued Edward. "Her aunt is to be buried today and she is nowhere to be found."

"Which is why we have come," said Erik. "Scarlet, I can assure you, is quite safe. She is at Gwyn Manor and is preparing for her aunt's funeral as we speak. I have come at her behest to collect her Lady Eliza and escort her to her final resting place."

"Gwyn Manor?" said Edward. "Why would she be there? It she all right?"

Erik motioned Jamen forward. "It seems that Scarlet no longer felt safe here and so she went to a place that she knew she would be."

Edward laughed. "Why would she not be safe here? And why would she come to you? Surely if she felt unsafe, she would have travelled home." He looked from one brother to the other.

This was it.

"You said once that you knew Lady Scarlet was not a Lady but a fake. That she had been engaged before and spoiled," said Jamen.

Sir Malcolm glowered at his son. "Edward, you didn't."

"Well…I…I didn't mean it like that," said Edward. "I'd had a bit too much to drink and— "

"You were right. Lady Greenwater's real name is Scarlet Mason. Her father used to be the merchant of Westfall before he left and you gentlemen arrived. And it is true that Scarlet had been engaged previously. To me."

173

Edward's eyes widened as did Sir Malcolm's.

"Scarlet and I were childhood sweethearts and that hasn't changed. Despite my abandoning her."

"You have been with her then?" asked Sir Malcolm.

Anger rippled through Jamen. He crossed his arms over his chest. "I will not dignify that with an answer suffice it to say, it is none of your business."

"Well it is *my* business." Edward shook his head a look of distress crossing his fine features. "As we are to be wed in a few days time."

"I'm afraid that is out of the question," said Jamen. "You see, Scarlet and I were wed yesterday at Gwyn Manor."

"How dare you," said Sir Malcolm. "And you, Lord Gwyn, how could you allow such a thing?"

"Allow?" said Erik. "I married them. Jamen and Scarlet should never have been parted in the first place. I was all too happy to see them finally wed as were the rest of my brothers and my sister."

Sir Malcolm took a step forward. "I'll see you ruined for this, Jamen Gwyn."

Jamen snorted. "I'd like to see you try. You think I give one sniff about you? I came here strictly out of respect for your son Edward, who seems to be the only honorable man in your family. He deserved to hear the truth from me. So you do your best, I've gone up against monsters far worse."

"Easy." Erik laid his hand on Jamen's arm. "I would suggest, Sir Malcolm, that you think carefully before you decide to go against my family. Rumors are already beginning to fly about this household. I would hate to see you without a home before the end of next year."

"What do you mean?" asked Edward.

"Lady Eliza was in your house when she was poisoned. Your manservant was involved. Some believe that the involvement of your family doesn't end with him. Eliza was a wealthy woman. Her money, passed now to Scarlet, would bolster your own coffers with Edward as Scarlet's husband."

"Lies," said Sir Malcolm. "You think that I would kill an old woman for money?"

"I think someone did." Erik looked around. "I don't see your older son, what's his name? Lyden?"

Sir Malcolm's face paled. "Lyden has gone on a trip with some friends. To see his grandmother in the south."

"I'm sure he has," said Erik. "And should *Lyden* decide to return to Westfall, I would very much like to speak with him."

Sir Malcolm swallowed. "He could be gone for quite some time."

"I'm patient," said Erik. "In the meantime, I will take the body of Lady Eliza so that we may return her to her home. You will have all of her things sent to Gwyn Manor as well as Lady Gwyn's items. And neither of you will speak an ill word about Lady Scarlet Gwyn or my brother Lord Jamen Gwyn, unless you want to find *yourselves* also needing to visit Grandmama in the south. Are we clear?"

Edward nodded vigorously. Guilt and shame hit Jamen.

"Oh! And one last thing," said Erik. "You tell your son Lyden and whomever he is working with, that Gwyn's have always lorded over Westfall and it will take a lot more than a few murders to get us out of Gwyn Manor."

With that, Erik and Jamen strode from the room and out to their horses.

"You should do some digging," said Erik as they led the cart carrying Lady Eliza away. "We need to find out who is behind these murders. Who wants us out of Westfall and what they are planning."

"Absolutely," said Jamen. "And why they are blaming vampires. I won't be able to do it alone."

"I'll send the twins."

"No," said Jamen. "Send Gerall, he's least likely to arouse suspicion when he questions people. Everyone likes him, and they vastly under estimate him."

Erik nodded.

*****

Scarlet stared out the window of Jamen's bedroom, their bedroom, knowing that the small family cemetery lay below. They'd brought Cosette home the day of her aunt's funeral and buried her next to Kellan. The grave marker was still being made, but she was glad to know that their first child would not be forgotten. She glanced at Jamen, who's brows furrowed in concentration and his tongue stuck out of his mouth slightly. He brushed a curl from his eyes and looked over at her. She smiled and reached for him.

"Don't move," he said.

"Sorry." She laughed.

His fingers worked feverishly across the parchment she'd bought him as a late Yuletide gift.

Over the past weeks they'd not left the manor house except for the one time to go into Westfall and another to go to Aunt Eliza's house to close it up for the winter. Belle and Chloe had been a wonderful comfort but watching them made her ache for a child of her own.

Gerall had arrived and inspected the bodies of Camille and Fredrick. They'd been killed by the same poison that had been used on Lady Eliza. So though they were all convinced Lyden had been behind it, they couldn't prove it.

Edward and his father had taken to shutting themselves up in their house for the last weeks. She still felt a pang of guilt for having hurt him so. Edward had only ever been kind to her.

On their trip into town Jamen had met with Father Ohana, the Mayor and his landlord to make sure it was well known that the Gwyns weren't going anywhere. When they'd walked arm in arm through the streets there had been stares and whispers, but Scarlet had held her head high, knowing that Jamen was hers.

Gerall was already making the rounds in town, trying to find out who was behind the attacks and murders. All in all, the Gwyn's were showing a united front.

Jamen set down his parchment and charcoal and Scarlet slid under the covers next to him. "What are you thinking about?" he asked.

"Just everything."

"That's a lot of things."

"Yes. It is."

He kissed her forehead and she laid her cheek on his shoulder and traced patterns over the scars on his chest.

"Do you think we'll be able to prove my aunt's murder?"

He held her tighter. "Don't you worry about that, Lady Gwyn. Soon enough you'll have a million other things to be doing."

"Oh really? And why is that?" she asked.

"Because we are going to open Gwyn Manor up."

Excitement raced through her. "Really?"

"I spoke with Gerall last night. If someone out there is trying to discredit us, we need to stop it. And the best way to do that is to open the doors to parties and entertaining... among other things."

"Other things?"

He gave her a sideways glance and a sly smile played across his face.

"What?"

"I've been thinking. Chloe has brought such laughter and happiness to Gwyn Manor. And though I am not the eldest I need to do my part. *We* need to do our part."

"Our part?"

"To carry on the Gwyn name and fill this whole manor house with life and laughter and half a dozen strong Gwyn men and several fair redheaded females. Chloe and Belle most certainly won't be here forever."

Scarlet smiled and Jamen slid his hand down between her thighs before locking his lips onto hers. She moaned into his mouth and rolled on top of him.

"Then let's start practicing," she whispered. "Over and over and over and over. It could take months before we get it right."

Her hips rocked back and forth making him grab the sheets and stare deep into her eyes. "I hope it does."

Zelle and The Tower

Fairelle Book Three

By Rebekah R. Ganiere

Ville DeFee, Fairelle

Autumn, 1210 A.D. (After Daemons)

CHAPTER ONE

With precision and speed, Flint pushed through the crowded street. He shivered and scowled at the silky touch of magick in the air. Pulling his cloak tighter about him, he kept his head down.

The footsteps of the king's guard pounded the cobblestone street a block behind.

"Find them!" the captain shouted.

It'd been a mistake to stop and ask for directions, but Flint had only been to Ville DeFee once, and with all the blasted brightly colored structures and sweet fruity smells he'd gotten turned around. Standing out amongst the slender, graceful fae, he lumbered through the streets.

His stomach growled as he passed a pastry store.

"Check every shop," a guard called.

A shrill call from a bright pink bird pierced Flint's ears, making him wince. He thanked the gods he hadn't been born in Ville DeFee.

Such brightness and merriment were overwhelming.

Dax shoved Flint sideways into a darkened alcove, away from an oncoming merchant carrying a basket full of blue fruit. He squeezed in next to Flint as the fragrances from the basket made his stomach growl once more. How long had it been since he'd eaten?

The merchant passed without a glance in their direction. Flint stuck his head out and scanned the area. The guards were still several shops away.

"We have to keep moving. The shop isn't too far." He darted onto the street.

"Do you really think this is a good idea?"

"No." He kept moving.

He was on a mission, and only the king himself would be able to stop him. He rounded a pale blue building and headed toward the end of the row. A fae youngling stopped skipping to stare at Flint.

He dropped his head again. His boots looked even filthier against the immaculate stone road. When was the last time he had washed them? Or taken a shower?

All of the days since leaving Tanah Darah and then Wolvenglen seemed to blend together into a horrible nightmare that he continually lived and relived. Only his hours spent in a drunken stupor and a couple of hazy memories with several tavern wenches broke up his personal hell. His gut clenched at the thought of seeing Snow as a vampire. Her skin, her eyes, her hair;, it was all different. She was different. Gone was the sweet younger sister that he'd tried to teach to dance. What she was now… was a creature he was bound to kill.

A screech and a crash yanked him from his dark thoughts.

"Excuse me," Dax said. "I'm so sorry."

Flint stopped and turned.

Dax threw apples into an overturned barrel as the shopkeeper looked on wide--eyed, mouth slack.

"Leave it." He scanned the street for the guard. People stopped to stare at Dax. Hood off, his shaggy blond head and tan skin screaming human.

Flint's skin itched and he clenched and unclenched his fists to keep from scratching his arms. The magick of the fae permeated everything. From the large, juicy, unnaturally colored and tasting foods to the highly polished, never dirty streets. It wasn't natural, it wasn't right.

Dax righted the barrel and stood.

Flint glanced skyward past the twinkling lanterns floating above. The moon had barely made an appearance but already the streets were crowding. They needed to get out of sight before night fell. Then the streets would be packed with fae, singing, dancing, and making merry on this Beginning of Spring Celebration.

"End of the street," Flint pointed. "Move it."

Dax nodded.

He hadn't wanted Dax to come along, but somehow the giant werebear had gotten the notion that he was responsible for Flint. After one fight together in which Dax saved his neck from being chewed on, and suddenly they were best of buddies.

In the past months though, Flint had come to appreciate Dax's company. Having lived with his six brothers and Snow for so long, the loneliness of being parted from them was not something he had thought about when storming out of the castle at Tanah Darah. And despite what he said, he liked Dax. Dax didn't talk too much and didn't pry. He kept his head straight and Flint's neck out of a noose.

They moved at a quickened pace until they reached the end of the street. Rounding a corner they found a smaller, darker area. The shops had already begun to close down for the night.

A bright peach building with purple awnings sported clusters of people coming and going. Shouting, laughing, and glasses clinking floated out the open windows of the pub. Flint's eye twitched and he licked his lips at the thought of getting a drink. The sounds of a flute lured him closer.

"Not here." Dax's large palm fell on Flint's shoulder.

He shook it off and continued on.

Drinking was not something he'd done regularly before. Now, it seemed more like a daily routine. What would father think? Flint pushed the pain aside and stomped towards to a mint green building. The worn red apothecary sign swayed in the breeze. A giant bluish tree wrapped the building in a hug. Vines in every color and variety snaked up the sides in a cocoon of protection.

Flint looked through the front window, but could see nothing except shelf upon shelf of bottles and herbs. He pushed open the door and two birds chimed a tune in unison. The scent of nature filled his nostrils. Roots and plants, herbs and flowers. It reminded him of Snow's cabinet where she kept her healing supplies. Again he was hit with a pang of guilt. But it didn't matter;, all that separated them would be gone soon.

A beautiful woman of about forty with light brown hair arranged bottles on shelves in the corner. She turned at the sound of the birds. Every surface of the shop was covered in jars, bags, and containers of various sundries. Flint removed his hood, as did Dax, and the woman started, dropping a bottle. The contents splashed on the floor, the glass shattering. A silent scream played on her red lips.

Flint threw up his hands. "I'm sorry to frighten you. I just need to speak to Lord Rondell and then we'll go."

The woman's green gaze lit on Dax. Horror remained solidly planted on her features. She stared at him without blinking.

Flint turned and gave Dax a questioning look. He shook his head and shrugged. Voices floated in from the street. If the woman screamed the guards would be alerted.

He turned to the woman. "Madame, I know we should not be here but—"

A beautiful young woman with bright blue eyes and rosy cheeks appeared from the rear of the store. "Stepmother, is there a prob—"

She scanned from Flint to Dax and then swiftly stepped around the counter and approached the woman, taking her by the arm.

"I'll take care of this. Why don't you go home while I clean up and close the shop."

The woman finally tore her gaze from Dax. She stared at the girl for a moment before yanking her arm away and composing herself. With another a sideways glance in Dax's direction, the woman nodded.

"Yes, of course you will. That's your job." She straightened her dress and hefted the hem so as not to step in the mess she'd made. "And if these two get caught in here, I'll not take the blame for it."

Tension thick as dragon-scale cracked in the air.

The girl nodded. "I understand."

The woman looked at Dax once more and then strode out.

When the door slammed shut, everyone sighed.

Quick as light the girl rushed to the entrance, magicked down the shades and dimmed the lights with a flick of her fingers. "Flint Gwyn. You sure do know how to make an entrance, don't you? Do you know what will happen if you're caught here?"

"I'll be thrown in prison."

"*I'll* be thrown in prison." The girl waved her hand and mumbled a word he couldn't hear. The smashed bottle reformed, and the liquid on the floor disappeared. She strode to it and put it on the shelf, then faced him again, a smile on her lips.

Flint relaxed. Coy girl. "Cinder. You're looking well. Last time I saw you, you appeared no more than a teen and I was no more than eight or nine."

"I was already in my late thirties back then. Good to know that I have aged well," she laughed. "I'm old enough to be your mother."

Taking several strides forward she reached out and embraced him with more strength than he thought her capable of. Pushing him to arms' length she looked up at him. "You used to pull my braid and hide my favorite book when we would come visit."

"And you would magick my pants so they wouldn't allow me to wear them."

"That was only after you tried to kiss me."

"Trust me, a disaster I would never dare to repeat. Besides, if I remember correctly you have a prince whose affection you were vying for. Did nothing ever come of that?"

She blushed. "Rome and I are just good friends."

He nodded and smiled. "Yes, I can see that."

Her fingers twitched. "Don't make me turn you into a mouse."

They laughed in unison and hugged again.

"Don't misunderstand me. I am happy to see you, but what in Fairelle are you doing here? You could've been seen."

"I'm looking for your father."

Cinder's eyes misted. "He is no longer with us, I'm afraid."

Flint's heart sunk. Lord Rondell had been his last hope.

"I'm sorry. I had not heard of his passing."

"It was quite sudden. We aren't exactly sure what happened. But he is in the Fade, with Mamette. And I know they are happy together."

"Of course." Flint blew out a heavy sigh. He'd come all this way. "Well then, it seems I've travelled for nothing. It was good to see you, Cinder. We should go before the soldiers come."

"Wait." She grabbed his cloak. "You came such a long way, what is it you need?"

"I doubt you can help, but thank you." He patted her hand and nodded to Dax. They replaced their hoods and turned.

Cinder harrumphed behind him. Arms crossed over her chest, she slid between Flint and the exit.

"You listen to me, Flint Gwyn. I am my father's daughter. And anything he could do, I can do. You look as though you haven't eaten in weeks, and your scent says you've bathed even less. You and your friend will sit at my counter, eat my food, use my washbasin and tell me why you came. For if you do not, I shall spell you and force you to. And I know you don't want that." With a wave of her hand, two chairs dragged themselves up to the shop counter.

She flashed him a brilliant smile and pointed to the chairs. Dax shrugged and headed for the counter. *Traitor.*
Flint wasn't sure if she was lying or not about the spell, but he was sure about one thing. She was definitely her father's daughter.

Thank you for taking the time to read
Jamen's Yuletide Bride

If you enjoyed the book, please take a moment to leave a review on your favorite retailer.

Look for the first books in the series:
Red the Were Hunter (Book One)
Snow the Vampire Slayer (Book Two)
&
Zelle and the Tower

To find out more about **Rebekah R. Ganiere** and *The Fairelle Series*, or her other Upcoming Releases, or to join her Newsletter for Swag and Freebies, Please connect with her in the following places:

BOOKS WITH A BITE

Newsletter: www.RebekahGaniere.com/Newsletter
Goodreads: www.Goodreads.com/VampWereZombie
Twitter: www.Twitter.com/VampWereZombie
Facebook: www.Facebook.com/VampiresWerewolvesZombies